Sav

By Steven Cleaver

Richmond, Indiana

Saving Erasmus

2018 Second Printing

Published by Steve Cleaver
Richmond, Indiana
www.stevecleaver.com
Printed in the United States of America

I'd like to acknowledge the community of believers in this world, those who understand that compassion is important, that human life is sacred and that the Arts are divine incarnate.

Thank you to **Bennett Ritchie** for the amazing cover art. What you created is unique, stand on it's own and honors the spirit of the novel. They say that you can't judge a book by its cover, but in this case, I'm happy if they do.

Table of Contents

Chapter One

In Which I Meet the Angel of Death

I did not expect to meet the Angel of Death while he was extricating himself from a washing machine. Actually I wasn't really expecting to meet the Angel of Death at all. Not this soon. Not in this place. Yet there he was, slowly unwinding himself from the open door of Dixie Manufacturer's finest front-loading commercial washer, twisting and turning and pulling his full body up over the rim and out onto the laundromat floor.

I guess no one really expects to see the Angel of Death in a laundromat, let alone climbing out of one of the machines. I suppose we all fantasize about something a bit more extravagant. The scene in Bergman's *The Seventh Seal* where Death is playing chess always resonated as realistic to me. In that scene, Death is dressed in black and hovers with a stark face over a very serious chess game. The surroundings are dark, and Armageddon appears to be looming on the horizon. It is quite ominous. I had always visualized the situation more like that, expecting there would be a little more edge to it. But expectations are tricky when it comes to Life and even I suppose to Death.

I admit that I was a bit startled. Most things need to be pulled out of a washing machine. I have never seen any item coming out under its own volition. Never, until now. I'd just dropped some coins into a dusty vending machine, selected a package of mints, and was waiting for them to drop when I first noticed him. I fidgeted at the catch bin in the machine with one hand and kept my eyes focused on the figure withdrawing himself from the washer at the other end of the building. It made me nervous, yet my curiosity was piqued. The scene brought to mind a monarch butterfly extracting itself somewhat wetly from the confines of the chrysalis, except this butterfly appeared quite experienced in his actions.

It was really just a mint that had brought me into the Quik Clean Laundromat. I had been traveling for a long time and had stopped next door at Agnes's Convenient, figuring that it would be the perfect place to get something for my dusty breath. I was meeting an important person for the first time, and I wanted to make a positive impression. Good breath is important.

Agnes's Convenient Store was one of those small little stores served by some barely traveled road and located on the outskirts of an inconsequential town. The signs posted in the windows had a slight discoloration to them from years and years of exposure to the sun. It was the kind of place where you would expect the food to be overpriced and out of date. Still, it looked immaculate.

The note on the door said, "Agnes is gone, Please return later." It was a small sign heavily taped to the inside of the glass door. I should have thought more about the note having been so securely posted, but I was in a hurry, and overlooked this as having any importance. So my quest brought me next door to the Quik Clean, where I would first encounter Death.

So how did I know this was Death? You must wonder that; I was questioning the experience myself. I have to be honest: most of my answer came from a gut feeling. A gut feeling I had learned to trust. There was energy to him, a not altogether negative energy, but something beyond the usual kind with which I come in contact. Electricity ran through my body and something inside resonated. It was an old feeling and one buried under years of layering, but the energy within it was potent. If you put me on a witness stand and asked for physical proof that this was indeed Death, I could not give it to you. Some experiences are like that. You just know.

He did look like an Angel of Death to me. He was tall, but it was not the exact measurement of his stature that was important, but rather the effect it had. He couldn't have been taller than seven feet because there was space between his head and the ceiling, but his body seemed to fill the room. His presence brought back a feeling I remember having as a child. Grownups weren't really so much larger than kids, but there was a confidence in the way they interacted and carried themselves that separated the adults from the children.

Death was dressed fully in black. Now you might say that this is a cliché; perhaps you want something more spectacular. Green would be nice. Chartreuse might even be even better. But I am merely a storyteller with a resolve to be true to the story. Black was his color. You picture what you want.

His face was invisible, hidden in the shroud of his cloak. The atramentous fabric hung over his body, rippling now and then, draping down to the floor, and girdling what appeared in outline to be wings. His arms were long and his bony hands extended from the edges of his sleeves. In retrospect, I would say that he was an amalgamation of all the representations of Death I had ever seen. Perhaps the closest depiction I could imagine was the third spirit in the movie *A Christmas Carol*. The 1952 Alistair Sims version. It's the best version.

Death stood erect in the middle of the laundromat floor. He shook his black covering, straightening himself, and knocked loose a few random unmatched socks and a handkerchief. He casually brushed the scattered remains of soap powder to the floor, creating a small ring of powdery flecks at the base of his cloak. He reached toward the ceiling to stretch, let out a big yawn and then turned his head to where I was standing.

I fumbled with the package, attempting to pull a mint out of it, and popped the round object that rolled out into my mouth. Unfortunately this turned out to be a small mass of undigested soap powder. I smiled tightly as I washed it around in my mouth and tried as hard as possible to become invisible, though I suppose nothing is invisible to Death, and invisibility is even more difficult when bubbles are forming at the corners of your mouth.

"Andrew," he said. I looked around the laundromat. It was deserted. I moved my right foot slowly back behind me as I considered a quick dive out the door. Perhaps there was another Andrew nearby. Maybe that Andrew would soon climb out of another washer or even the dryer.

"Andrew Benoit!" This time there was a hint of annoyance in his pronunciation. I tried to ignore the call, but it was perfectly obvious he was saying my name. His voice reverberated in the laundromat. I guess there could have been another Andrew Benoit around, but since I was alone, it was hard to disregard the fact that I was his focus. Death was trying to get my attention, I was ignoring him, and even Death gets irritated. As he spoke, washer doors flung open, a volley of mismatched socks flew by my face, and I could see used dryer sheets clinging in a corner. One random argyle sock fluttered past my head. It looked familiar.

I stood facing the giant figure, transfixed with a mix of fear and awe. *God won't give me more than I can handle,* I thought. I stood my ground.

"I . . . I am Andrew Benoit," I replied, raising one eyebrow quizzically and hoping that he just wanted something simple like directions. My heart was beating rapidly and I dropped the package of mints to the floor. Nothing in my seminary studies had prepared me to encounter Death. Not like this at least.

"Can I help you?" I asked. I had worked customer service for a summer and learned how to diffuse quickly what might become difficult situations. Now, having considered the options of fight or flight, I figured that a third choice would be best. When Death calls your name it's wise to be helpful.

"I am the Angel of Death," he said. Okay, my guess had been accurate. I generally take the word of any large figure that knows my name. It's just common sense.

"What do you want from me?" I asked. I looked up into the faceless void, mints scattered at my feet, a slight tremble in my legs. I am not one for conflict. I would rather avoid a situation that calls me to confront. Simple things like poor service or pushy people on the subway cause me to tighten up, and this was bigger than those. I was facing Death and it was quite possible that I was going to have to put up resistance. Death meant business. He wasn't carrying a chessboard.

"I am going to wipe out the whole town of Erasmus in a week," he said, with a casual air that belied the significance of his words.

This was important news for me. Erasmus was the small town I was headed for when I stopped for a mint. I'd been offered the job of pastor in the local church, a one-year appointment I was eager to finish with and move on. My seminary scholarship required that I work for the first year in a small, less sought-after community, and from all the information I could gather, it seemed that Erasmus had been a particularly hard place to work. I had resigned myself to this fact, comforted by the underlying knowledge that I would soon be headed to bigger and better things. Erasmus seemed like a place that people came from but would never intentionally head to.

"You are going to wipe out the whole town of Erasmus?" I asked. It's best, I think, to be clear when questioning Death. My expectations for the future were changing quickly and I needed clarification.

"Yes," he said. "I will be returning for them in a week."

"Is this God's work?"

"Yes," he replied and then paused. "God has been watching this town for a long time."

"Why would God watch Erasmus?" I asked, incredulous. "It's a nothing town. Why would God want them destroyed?"

I couldn't imagine anyone spending very much time examining the town of Erasmus. It was simply one more town like any other between the coasts, a dot in the middle of a line called a road. Erasmus was geographically superfluous. You forget thousands of towns like Erasmus on the way to one place that you remember.

"They have been losing faith," Death replied nonchalantly as he flicked a small, hardened particle of powdered soap off of his shoulder. It landed on one of the red plastic folding tables and then rolled on to the floor.

"Soon their faith will be gone."

"So God called you?"

"Yes," he replied. "Once a certain number of people in a given community lose their faith, it triggers a natural signal. I get an automatic call. After that, God has nothing to do with it anymore. God stopped being involved with all that destruction stuff long ago. Too heartbreaking."

Well, that's good, I thought. *God seems to have turned the whole dying process over to a hired hand. No more fuss or worry about making the decision.* I suppose I really couldn't blame God for being exhausted what with the constant covenant making and covenant breaking that went on. Human beings certainly had not made their Creator's life easy. No wonder God stepped out of the picture. Sparrows are easier.

"So you're going to destroy the town in one week because a certain percentage of people have lost faith?

"Exactly," he replied.

"Why tell . . . me?" I asked. Why was it necessary that I know? I figure Death pretty much works on his own. I have heard stories of people who have premonitions and visions, but this was not the case here. The Angel of Death was relying on me. I was getting thrown the ball in the last minutes of the fourth quarter and up until this point I hadn't even been playing the game. No, I didn't even know the game.

"I have to pick someone," he said. "They get one last chance. I get to call one prophet." Death's voice became very serious. "You're the one I selected."

"Is this because I went to seminary?"

"No, Andrew. That was just part of your path." He paused. "Actually I picked many. But," he said as he pointed to the empty laundromat, "you are the only one to show up."

Great, I thought. *A dying man gets a last phone call and I'm it. Thanks, Death. Publishers*

Clearing House randomly selects Mary Beth Finster from East Albatross, Kansas, to win a million dollars and what do I get? Death and the promise of unemployment.

"I never get picked for anything."

"No, Andrew. You never get picked for what you think you should have. That is different."

"But I'm not a prophet," I said. "I mean, I really don't think I have the proper training." I'd been called many things in my life, some of which I would rather not see in print, so I will let you ascribe your own colorful and descriptive adjectives and nouns. "Prophet" had never been thrown out in any kind of verbal exchange. *There are no more prophets,* I thought, but even on the remote chance that there were, I was certain I was not one.

"Anyone can be a prophet," Death replied.

Well, throw the theories in the last paragraph out. I am a prophet. The prophets were a diverse bunch. Jonah, Jeremiah, Elisha, Deborah, Elijah. I wasn't so certain I was of their caliber, and now, I'd been called to save a hopeless town. Stuck in some Godforsaken place, and Death has just informed me that it will be destroyed in a week. So much for job security.

“Then you sent the plagues after the bus?” I asked.

“That was God,” he replied. ”I’m not really big on plagues. Not as signs, at least.”

“But the bus . . . you knew I would turn around?”

“I never know,” he shrugged. “As I said, I called many, but only you showed up.”

Save Erasmus. This was the call. I didn’t even know Erasmus. I had just arrived, and I wasn’t really infatuated with the little I saw.

Save Erasmus? I had hardly ever been able to save anything. I had trouble keeping my checkbook balanced. Once I had found a baby bird in the back yard. The bird was obviously not well.

“What will you do with it?” asked my father.

“I don’t know, Dad,” I said. “I just don’t want him to die.” The bird died after two days. I cried for longer. And a bird is small compared to a town, even a town like Erasmus.

“But how do I save a town?” I asked.

"I do not know of your way," he said. "You must find that in yourself."

It was customary in the Bible for all of the residents of a faithless town to dress in sackcloth to signal a change of heart and seek God's forgiveness. This was not an easy task to accomplish. I pictured myself organizing the men, women, children, and livestock of Erasmus into groups of remorseful supplicants. The men and women I could handle. A little reason, some hellfire and brimstone and perhaps a few pictures of Armageddon, and they would be convinced. The children would be tougher. Perhaps promises of increased television and new cell phones would seal the deal. The livestock worried me most. How would I talk an obstinate bull into putting on a sackcloth outfit? "Look," I would have to say. "It's all the rage. The cows love it. And the matadors are raving about sackcloth over in Spain." The livestock would be tough but the cats would be impossible. I think I'd just bribe them to leave with a load of kibble.

"I have a week, then?" I asked.

"Yes."

"And then you will return?

"Yes." Death was nothing if not succinct.

"Where will you be then?" I asked. I am not one who likes surprises. Just tell me outright, put your cards on the table, so I know what to play.

"You will know," he said.

"How? How will I know?"

"You will know," he said again, with annoyance in his voice that reminded me again that I was after all speaking with Death, and it probably was not a good idea to get him angry.

"Do you always come and go through washing machines?" I asked. It really wasn't that odd, actually. I remember reading *The Lion, the Witch, and the Wardrobe* when I was a child. The children in the Narnia books find a magic kingdom behind a door in the back of the closet. A washer is not much different from a closet. Both were spaces in which you put clothes. Clearly this morning was a good time to suspend disbelief.

"Not always," he replied. "But often. I use the broken ones; that way I don't have to worry about getting wet."

Fair enough. The washing machine that he had come out of had a sign that read "Broken. Don't Use. No Money Returned If You Do," taped to the glass. There was always at least one broken washing machine in every laundromat I'd ever been in.

"Now I must go." He sifted through the pockets of his black garment and produced a handful of quarters. "Three dollars for a load. This is getting ridiculous," he sighed. He placed the coins in the slot and leapt deftly up and into the open hole.

"Please," he said, "close the door and turn the controls to gentle."

I reached up to close the door but he scrunched his head back out. "And no soap," he said with a wry smile. Even Death has a sense of humor.

I nodded in acknowledgment, closed the door gently, and turned the knob to the gentle cycle. I pushed the buttons and the giant washer began to spin. Death was right; he knew how to disconnect the water and initiate the spin cycle so he wouldn't get wet. I could see his black covering slip and twirl and watched as Dixie Manufacturer's finest sucked the Angel of Death into its mystical vortex.

I realized after he was gone that I still had many questions for him. It was like when you leave a job interview and you suddenly realize that you forgot to ask about benefits. The questions swam in my head. How can Death be in more than one place at a time? Which came first, Death or Life? Do you like your job? What really happened to Marilyn Monroe, Amelia Earhart, Jimmy Hoffa, Judge Crater, Anastasia, and Elvis? What occurred on that grassy knoll?

The Angel of Death was gone, and I experienced suddenly a vast emptiness in the laundromat. Those had been big shoulders that had vanished in the turn of a rotor. I was left alone with the immediate call of my task: Save Erasmus.

Save a whole town. Me. Andrew Benoit. Naturally, I felt rather overwhelmed by this unexpected development. I was alone. No one had witnessed my interaction with the Angel of Death. Only the soap particle outline on the floor, the discarded socks, and the dwindling electricity in my body affirmed my experience. My mind slowly stilled, and I became aware of the quiet that surrounded me. Mints lay scattered at my feet. Bubbles were spewing softly from my mouth. Death had just visited me and told me that he was going to destroy a town if I did not convince the inhabitants to repent.

Again I imagined preparing people, cows, and chickens in sackcloth and small signs in order to avoid God's wrath. I visualized preaching a moving sermon that brought grown men to tears, kept children awake, and convinced stubborn bulls to wear burlap. There would be a lot of work to do in the week ahead. This was not going to be easy.

It was only ten o'clock in the morning, and already I had been warned by Death that Armageddon was coming in a week. I considered my options. I'd stopped in the laundromat on my way to meet Mrs. Primrose Davenport, and it seemed that the best course would be to keep the appointment. After all, I had to start somewhere.

I didn't know it yet, but this day was only going to get worse.

Chapter Two

The Road Less Traveled

I scooped up the scattered mints with my hand. As I was dropping them into the waste can, I picked one out and flicked the particle of dust off its surface, looked around to see if anyone had entered the laundromat and, certain the area was devoid of humans, put the mint into my mouth. My breath was of uncertain quality, and a little bleach from the floor could only help.

Business was sure slow on a Saturday morning in early May. Maybe the residents did their laundry in a stream in Erasmus. I pictured the townspeople pounding rocks on top of various garments while the water flowed underneath. I was open to options. After all, I'd just met the Angel of Death.

The sun was overhead as I walked into the parking lot. The sign was still on the door at Agnes's Convenient Store: the store was still closed. *Agnes must be ill,* I thought. *Or perhaps she's having an early morning rendezvous with a mystery man.* Whatever it was, Agnes's store was anything but convenient on this morning.

I swung my backpack onto my back. The pack was small and held only the essentials that I would need on this spiritual journey: some clothes, a Bible, my camera, and a few pounds of good coffee. The rest of my belongings I'd donated to charity. I was embracing the ascetic life. So far the results had been troubling.

I walked out of the parking lot and made my way across Highway 35, which was the main road in and out of town. A sign read, "Welcome to Erasmus. Population 510."

Welcome? I hardly felt welcome. Frustrated, maybe. Anxious, definitely. Confused? Oh, yes. I looked down the outbound road longingly.

So how did I end up here to begin with? The truth is, Erasmus would never have been on my list of preferred destinations. Coming here wasn't among the affirmations that I wrote out each day. I would never have predicted that early May would have found me in this place. St. Augustine's Seminary requirements, Robert Frost, the Marx

Brothers and a baseball brought me. It was that simple.

All right, it really wasn't that simple.

*

St. Augustine's Seminary and St. Monica's Finishing School for Girls were founded in the early 1900s to train young men to be ministers and young women to be ministers' wives. St. Monica's was bankrupt by the early 1950s, but St. Augustine's had flourished and now prepared both men and women to minister to a suffering world.

My presentation of "The Missing Letter on the Gutenberg Press and How It Has Affected the Modern Church" had been highly lauded and granted me top status in my class. As a result, I'd been offered a place at St. Exupery's Cathedral, a large church advantageously situated on the East Coast overlooking the ocean, with a congregation that included many celebrities.

The ceremony where post-graduate placement decisions are announced is eagerly anticipated each year. It takes place in Montanus

Hall, named for St. Montanus, an early martyr, and known fondly to students as "Monte Hall." But as I walked through the voluminous halls of St. Augustine's I was conscious only of uncertainly and indecision.

"Hey, Benoit!"

I turned around and saw Michael Servetus striding in my direction. Michael had entered seminary after first graduating from medical school. He and I had argued periodically about one of my favorite comedy teams, the Three Stooges. Michael thought they should only have one combined footprint site at Grauman's Chinese Theatre and I felt they should each have one. Though he had been a difficult pupil for the professors, constantly disagreeing with many of their beliefs, I found him to be one of the most engaging students at St. Augustine's. He had been circulating among the graduates before hailing me.

"Where did you decide to go?" he quizzed.

"Well, I'm still not certain."

"Not certain, old man? You're going to have to announce it shortly! Why, I'd have thought you'd have decided long ago."

"I've got a lot to think about."

"What's to think about?" he laughed. "St. Exupery's is the goose that lays the golden egg! By the way, aren't you going to ask me?"

"Sure, Servetus," I said. "Where are you headed?"

"I'm going to work at a small publishing house for a while. Lyon Press. Not sure I was cut out for this ministering stuff, like you. You were made for it."

Made for ministry. It was a tag I had worn proudly all of my life. Long ago, I had determined that I was going to be a man of faith and good works. That way there could be no question about my calling.

"Yes, I suppose I was," I replied.

My work at St. Augustine's had been exemplary. I had demonstrated an investigative nature and an inquisitive mind. So why was I so uncertain as to where my next move should take me? Well, the truth was, I always had difficulty making choices. Even as a child, when my family went to Howard Johnson's for ice cream, my father, mother, and older brother, Jamie, would easily select from the multitude of flavors while I stood trying to figure out what I wanted until someone shouted, "C'mon, kid, hurry up!" from the back of the line. Often whatever flavor I selected would not taste as good as I expected, but at least it was only ice cream. This choice was different.

"Remember, Andrew," Michael said in the tone of a trickster who has the master stumped, "he who hesitates is last."

I stared back at him, waiting, knowing that if I allowed a little time to pass Servetus would, for a brief moment, believe he had won.

"Mae West. Too easy."

"Darn!" he said. "You know those comedians too well."

"Like family," I said. "They're like family."

"Speaking of which," he continued, "is anyone from your family coming to graduation?

"Ah, no," I said.

"Well," he laughed, "you can share some of mine. I have more than I need."

"Sure," I said quickly. "Hey, listen, I have to go."

"Okay. Good luck with your decision. I know you'll make a good one."

I wasn't so certain. I was waiting for someone to shout, "C'mon, kid," but the halls were silent.

The thing was, just minutes before I ran into Servetus I'd been absolutely certain where I was going. But that was before I'd encountered Robert Frost and Professor Anderson.

* * *

Professor Archimedes Anderson was one of St. Augustine's leading academics. He enlivened his classes by performing the parts of ancient characters in historical tales. Once he had performed the role of St. Benedict, reenacting the scene where Benedict is nearly poisoned by the men in the monastery, and another of him rolling in nettles. Professor Anderson even used real nettles, which meant the class ended a bit early that day. I loved his classes because he brought religion to life.

In addition to being one of St. Augustine's leading teachers, Professor Anderson was also my mentor. He continually challenged me to think outside the box.

"Andrew," he once said as I handed him my too-well-researched paper that carefully documented how Methuselah spent each of his 969 years, "God does not live in these." He pointed to his ceiling-high bookshelves, crammed with thousands of literary and reference works. "Or in this," he said as he tapped me on the head with my rolled-up paper. "God lives in the people. All the people."

"I know," I replied.

"You think you know, Andrew," he said. "But you must know it here." He pointed to my heart. "Your journey must take you from here," he said as he touched my forehead with his finger, "to here." His finger traced a line the air that ended at the point of my heart.

"I think I am there," I told him.

"That is the problem. One day, you will not think it. You will know it."

* * *

Professor Anderson's room was in the basement of Holscher Hall. He said he liked to believe that he was in the Essene caverns. As I walked toward his room now, I heard screaming.

I knocked on the heavy wooden door. Trash and recycling covered the hallway. Papyrus scrolls were stuffed into bags and a broken ossuary had been tossed into the recycling bin. "Professor Anderson?" I called. From behind the door I could hear vibrant expletives being shouted. Professor Anderson was coloring the air with Latin, Greek, and Hebrew and saturating the atmosphere with words such as Sheol, Baol, and Hades. "Professor Anderson!" I pounded a bit harder.

"YES!" I heard, then, "yes, yes," again, the tone of voice changing from annoyance to regained confidence. "Come in."

Professor Anderson was busily dabbing a large papyrus scroll on his desk with paper towels. Coffee dripped from it onto the floor. He looked up. "I'm sorry, Andrew," he said. "I hope I didn't frighten you."

"Well no," I said. "Is something wrong?"

He looked at me, and in his eyes I could see both wisdom and the beginnings of tears. Then I looked more closely at the scroll on his desk, and my eyes widened with amazement.

"Wow! That's a great copy of the Nag Hammurabi!"

"It's not a copy," he replied sadly and continued dabbing at the parchment.

"Oh," I responded feebly. "Can I help?"

"No," he said. "It's pretty dry now. Hopefully, it'll be okay." He glanced from the scroll to me, then to the clock on his office wall. "You must be headed to the ceremony," he said. "You have decided?"

"Are you sure everything is all right?" I asked, gesturing at his desk.

"Yes, I'm used to this," he said. "But you, where did you decide to go?"

"St. Exupery's," I told him triumphantly.

"Oh," he replied. Professor Anderson had shepherded me through the seminary by constantly redirecting my energy. If I came to him seeking advice, he would ask me to clarify what I was looking for.

"St. Exupery's will give me everything I've always wanted," I told him.

"What have you always wanted?"

"Well, to be in a big church where there's lots of opportunity. It's a prestigious post. Everyone says I should take it.

"Is that why you did this?"

"I don't know," I said. "Is there anything wrong with wanting those things?"

"It was my understanding that your scholarship required you to work in a less desirable community for the first year."

"The rules don't exactly exclude St. Exupery's. The wording is pretty vague." This was true.

"Ah. I see."

"You think it's wrong?"

"It's not a question of what I think," he replied. "It's a question of what's right in your heart. But sometimes it pays to choose the road less traveled."

"That will make all the difference?" I laughed.

"Perhaps." He wasn't laughing. "So all this time you've spent here, wasn't it about helping people?"

"Well, I do want to help people," I said. "But it seems like everyone else I knew is getting high paying jobs and is doing better."

"Doing better can be helping people." He paused. "I wouldn't have said anything, but I know they need help right now."

"Who?" I asked. "Where?"

"Erasmus," he replied.

"Erasmus!" I hooted. "That's the road *never* traveled!"

"Andrew," he intoned, his soft eyes glaring intently, "there's no need for sarcasm."

"Sorry."

"Someday that will get you into trouble."

"I'm sorry," I said. "It was just so funny."

"Why?"

"*Erasmus?* It's the middle of nowhere!"

"Oh, Andrew. You're being overly dramatic. If God has a purpose, God will provide. There are people there who need you. But the choice is yours. You must decide." He refocused his gaze on the scroll, began dabbing at it, then looked up once more. "Soon."

I walked out the door and stumbled on the trashcan, causing a small silver chalice to crash to the floor.

Hesitantly I moved down the cavernous halls of St. Augustine's, surrounded by the various scenes of martyrdom depicted in the paintings that lined the walls. The painted eyes of the saints and martyrs followed me as I walked: St. Benedict, St. Patrick, St. Hildegard of Bingen, St. Francis of Assisi, and St. Philip. Pancras and Stephen had been stoned to death. Montanus and Heschyius of Antioch were drowned. There was a large portrait of Prisca looking up at a lion. Surely there was a fine line between martyrdom and common sense?

Erasmus vs. St. Exupery's. No contest! I headed down the path back to my apartment and dropped my books on the chair on top of a pair of pants, a sandwich, and some old newspapers. Wasn't it fair to choose the fancier place? I'd worked hard to earn that offer, and wouldn't exactly be disregarding my scholarship agreement, not technically at least. Was it wrong to turn away from Erasmus simply because they had so little to offer?

"God," I prayed. "Show me the way."

No more than a second later, a well-hit baseball flew through the open window, careened off the spice rack, bounced on the table, rolled across the floor and ended its prophetic journey by colliding loudly with my video cabinet. One video was dislodged by the force and fell to the floor.

I picked up the baseball, a Chicago Cubs ball that had been signed by the World Series Team. The video on the floor was The Marx Brothers comedy "*Go West.*"

Go West! I'd prayed for a sign, but was this it? If so, west could mean only one thing: Erasmus. St. Exupery's lay to the east. Erasmus! It was almost heretical to consider. Other questionable towns had come and gone off the placement list, but no one in the history of St. Augustine's had ever selected Erasmus. I knelt and lifted the video, assigning it all the importance and weight Atlas had given the world when he placed it on his shoulders.

"C'mon, mister, hurry up!"

From my window I saw a group of children staring back up at me.

"Throw us the ball!"

There was a round-headed boy, a girl with black hair, and an outfielder surrounded by a cloud of dirt. Earlier that day, I'd stood waiting for an adult to yell "c'mon, kid, hurry up," at my childhood self from the back of the ice cream line. Instead, a child was yelling "c'mon, mister, hurry up," at my adult self. What did the old adage say—something about from the mouths of babes? I tossed the ball down to the waiting crowd.

* * *

Monte Hall was filled to bursting with students and throngs of parents who sat, proudly, in the back of the auditorium. This was the premiere event of the year for seeing and being seen. I adjusted my cap and gown and lined up with my fellow students, and when the signal was given we walked to our seats at the front of the auditorium. Bernard had taped a masking tape message on his cap that read "In God We Trust"; Gerald wore vestments that had been handed down for generations.

The ceremony began. I was completely distracted. Each time I mentally practiced calling out "St. Exupery!" the word "Erasmus!" popped into my head. It wasn't just Professor Anderson. It wasn't just the ball. There was also the feeling that in abiding by the letter rather than the true intent of my scholarship agreement, I'd be doing something not quite right in my heart.

Professor Roy Hinkley stood at the podium. The moment everyone had been waited for had arrived. "Ladies and gentlemen, I am proud to present this year's graduating class of St. Augustine's!" The crowd applauded loudly. "As I call out the name of the graduating senior, the student will announce the placement they have selected."

"Elaine Robinson," Professor Hinkley called out.

"Santa Anna," she replied. There was a pause and a small round of applause. Any town with Santa in it was desirable for two reasons. One, it was good to have a saint on your side. Two, I find that towns with names like that were usually in sunnier climates. I would have loved to go to a nice place right on the ocean.

"Daniel Frostflake."

"Santa Echeverria!" Another saint name. The thought of warmth and sun again entered my mind. Daniel was the kind of student who did everything without question. This Daniel would have walked into the lion's den simply because it was a course requirement. His theological and spiritual journey had ended once he exited the womb.

I sat somewhat agitated in my seat while the names continued to be called. One after another my classmates walked to the front and accepted their package of papers.

"Andrew Benoit."

There was a pause. The crowd turned in their seats to watch as I stood up in the back of the room. The words caught in my throat. I thought of the large congregation I could be working with. The sound of the beautiful new pipe organ, the throngs of listening parishioners, and the call of the ocean danced in my mind.

"Erasmus," I called.

The room became devoid of sound. The crowd turned again, stunned, to look at me.

"Andrew, I couldn't hear your choice clearly." The crowd was still staring. Perhaps the vichyssoise served at the banquet had been overheated and was affecting their hearing. Maybe I had sneezed. Perhaps I was joking.

"Erasmus!" I called out again, louder. I looked at the faces of the parents and my fellow students. Two hundred deer staring into the spotlights at a football stadium would have appeared less surprised.

I trekked up to the front, my black gown flowing as it waved past the shocked gazes of the crowd. I would have liked to explain about the baseball, but I wasn't so certain people would understand. There's a fine line between faith and insanity, and I wasn't at all sure at that moment which side I was on.

* * *

We had a week after the gala before we would leave for our new homes. For days I searched for other signs that I'd made the right choice, but found none. I threw balls in the window and only ended up breaking my cookie jar.

"Nothing's set in stone," Michael Servetus told me. "You can always change your mind. I know my church still has a place."

"Yeah, I know," I said. "I just don't think I can."

During this time, graduates received correspondence regarding their assignments. Elaine Robinson had a visit from elder members of her church; Michael Servetus received a lengthy contract that included a well-written welcome letter. I had a tattered copy of an old, dusty application form, given to me by Professor Anderson. A Mrs. Davenport was the sole contact name in Erasmus. I took a deep breath and dialed her number.

"Hello?" Her tone was uncomfortably icy.

"Mrs. Primrose Davenport? I asked.

"Mrs. Davenport will do," she answered briskly.

"My name is Andrew Benoit," I said.

“I am really quite busy.”

“I’m the seminary student that you requested,” I said, a bit flustered at her lack of friendliness.

“Oh,” she said, then paused. “Oh, this must be some sort of mistake.”

I stood quietly, holding the phone and waiting.

“I suppose we did request a pastor,” she relayed. “But that’s years ago now.”

This is the sort of moment when religious training comes into play. I wanted to throw a few select expletives into the conversation but realized they would not exactly sanctify the situation.

“Well, I’ve been assigned your town. Are you telling me that you don’t have a job for me?” I asked, taking a deep, hopeful breath. Here was my chance. *Come on, Primrose,* I thought; *give me the break I need.* The warm ocean air was calling.

“Well . . .” there as a long pause. “We do need a pastor,” she said.

With these words my hopes of freedom in a sunny Promised Land were shattered. Erasmus needed a pastor, and I’d chosen Erasmus. “Are you sure you want me?" I asked her, unwilling to give up that recent faint hope.

"Yes. Yes," she said. "I believe that this will work." She hesitated a moment. "Benoit. Did you have ancestors aboard the Mayflower?"

"No," I replied. I couldn't remember anyone ever discussing the Benoit heritage in glowing terms. If a Benoit did come over on the Mayflower, he must have stowed away. More likely, a Benoit would have hijacked the ship if possible. My paternal ancestry was full of thieves, reprobates, and black sheep. White sheep were the oddballs.

Mrs. Davenport questioned me for a while about my family and connections. Many of my answers were met with long stalled "Oh's" that seemed to reflect disappointment. It seemed I was not Mrs. Davenport's precise cup of tea. She was accustomed to English Earl Grey, whereas I'm more of a generic herbal Green. She somehow managed to convey the impression that she would not want me sitting on her furniture, even if she had plastic slipcovers on it.

"Come at eleven AM Saturday," she said.

"Yes, ma'am," I responded.

"Wear a suit," she said.

"Yes, ma'am."

"A *clean* suit."

"Yes ma'am," I replied yet again. I was biting my tongue as I spoke.

"And if your shoes have any dirt on them, come in the back door."

Chapter Three

Pelted with Plagues

Clean shoes. It seemed that this would be easy enough to accomplish . . . until I saw the bus that was to take me to Erasmus, that is. It was filthy. I stood in the main parking lot, my backpack neatly packed and my goodbyes completed, and studied the two buses parked side by side. It appeared that the other graduates would be whisked to their destinations by sleek charter bus. The Lady Line was known for excellent service, plush seats, and gourmet meals. A finely groomed driver greeted the students, accepted their belongings with a smile, and assisted them onto the vehicle. The bus to Erasmus, on the other hand, appeared stranded. The driver was busy looking under the hood at a steaming front engine. I walked over to him.

"Hi," I said, tapping the driver on the shoulder. He turned slowly to speak.

"Hey," he replied. "What can I do for you?"

"I'm Andrew Benoit. I'm going to Erasmus."

"Let me just check that," he said as he pulled a greasy list out of his back pocket. He scrutinized it for a few minutes.

"Benoit. Benoit. Ah, there ya are." He pulled a pen from behind his ear and checked my solitary name off. He crumpled the list and put it back in his pocket.

"You're Bill?" That was the name on his Tiger Lines shirt.

"No," he replied. "We only have one shirt. Got to share it. Name's Sam, actually."

"Hi, Sam."

"Hey, he said. "You got a radio?"

"No, sorry. I gave most of my belongings away."

"Ah, that's okay. The radio's broken but we can play license plate games, I guess. It's a pretty long ride."

The middle of nowhere takes along time to get to. Somewhere is closer. Always.

"How long?" I asked.

"Ah, let's say ten hours."

At this moment, Servetus walked up behind me.

"Benoit, you sure you're going to make it in this?"

"Not comfortably," I replied. "It's a ten-hour drive."

"Hey, I'd say it's a sign, Andrew. You can come with us. Save this poor guy a drive."

"You think?"

"Sure," he said. "You yourself said that Erasmus wasn't too sure of having you. Just say you changed your mind."

"But the baseball," I reminded him. "The sign?"

"C'mon, Andrew, it's just a baseball.

"You're right. Hey, Sam, my plans might be changing."

"Whatever. Just give me a call. I'll be here for a while," he said. "Here, take my card." He reached down again into the engine with a screwdriver. "Wouldn't be the first time."

"Thanks." I slipped his card into my wallet and walked across the lot to where the other bus was idling. Elaine Robinson was dressed in a wedding gown, having married Ben Braddock earlier in the day. They boarded the bus and sat in the back.

"Name?" the bus driver asked as he reached his hand out to shake mine. "I'm Jonas Grumby."

"Benoit," I said. "Andrew Benoit. I don't think I'm on your list."

Jonas checked his meticulous list.

"You're right. No problem," he said. "Happens all the time. After all, look what you'd be missing. New turbocharged bus. Video games. Choice of movies. Welcome."

"It's a sign, Andrew," Servetus said, as he patted me on the shoulder.

"I guess."

"C'mon kid, it's an easy choice," laughed Jonas. "Heck, it's only a three-hour trip."

"Sure," I said, as I looked over at Sam and his hapless vehicle, now listing slightly to one side. It happens all the time.

I stepped onto the bus. The seats were incredibly soft and surrounded me with the plush affirmation of a correct choice. I settled in for a comfortable trip. Servetus sat behind me.

"See, Andrew? It all worked out," he said.

Jonas Grumby's voice came over the loudspeaker. "Welcome, ladies and gentlemen. Please let the attendant know if you need anything by pressing the red buzzer above your head. Otherwise, settle in for a comfortable ride." He started the bus, and the sleek vehicle glided out of the parking lot.

"Man, Servetus, you were right," I said, but he was already asleep. I slid back in my ergonomically correct seat and planned the next step of my journey. The packing toils of the past weeks had taken their toll, and I drifted easily into a delicate slumber, only to be awakened by a gentle pinging against the sides of the bus. The skies were clear except for small swarms of bugs.

"Gnats," I said. "Hey, Servetus, we're being swarmed by gnats."

Servetus was just waking up. He squinted one eye to look at me. "Gnats? You sure?"

"Yeah," I said. "Look out the window." By now the swarm had increased, and loud bangs sounded against the metal sides of the bus.

"They'll go away. It was a wet spring." He was about to place his head back down on his pillow when a new sound began, louder and heavier than the gnats.

"Frogs!" I yelped. "It's frogs!"

The amphibious bombardment woke up the whole bus. Windows were slammed shut to ward off incoming bodies of the airborne animals. Rain had already created a small river in the aisle. A few frogs hopped around in the water.

"We're being pelted with pestilence," Christina Celfiore screamed from the back of the bus.

"More exactly," Servetus corrected, "plagues. We're being pelted with plagues."

"Servetus," I said, "it's me. This is because of me."

"What? What does it have to do with you?"

"I have to go to Erasmus."

"Andrew," he said. "I hardly think so. Surely there's a reasonable explanation. Maybe the frogs were chasing the gnats."

"No." I looked out the window. Dark clouds were forming in the sky. Frogs and gnats bounced off the window.

"Ladies and gentlemen," announced Jonas, "please fasten your seatbelts. It's going to be a bumpy evening."

At that moment another animal form joined the gnats and the frogs. Locusts. Huge locusts were hitting the side of the bus with increasing force. I pressed the red buzzer above my head.

"It's me," I shouted. "It's me. I have to go back!"

The bus braked easily with the smooth action one would expect from the Lady Line. Most of the students were busy praying for help and didn't appear to notice my confession.

"Servetus," I said, as I grabbed my backpack from the open overhead bin, "I have to go to Erasmus."

"Do what you have to, Andrew," he stated, as he brushed a locust carcass off my pack. "If you think it's about you, maybe it is."

I hurried up the aisle as even louder banging sounds came from the sides of the bus. Cats and dogs. This was definitely a sign.

"You know what you're doing?" Jonas said, as I arrived at the front of the bus.

"I have to get off, Jonas. This is my fault. God is calling me."

"If you say so, little buddy." He opened the door, and I rode a wake of rainwater, gnats, frogs, and locusts out onto the shoulder. My fellow seminarians waved to me as the bus glided back into the road. The sky was clear. The plagues had abated.

I spent the rest of the afternoon picking gnats and locusts out of my hair as I hiked back to St. Augustine's.

Sam still stood in the exact same spot front of his bus as I arrived in the parking lot. A copy of *Transmissions for Dummies* lay at his feet.

"Man, what happened to you?" he asked, looking up from the engine. "Looks like you had a rough trip. Guess those Lady Line buses aren't all they're cracked up to be, eh?"

"It wasn't the bus, Sam. It was God. I have to go to Erasmus."

"Whatever you say. If that's true, I wish your God had fixed this hours ago. Ah, well, no harm done." He wiped the sweat from his forehead with a handkerchief and placed it in his pocket.

"You can take your stuff up and put it in the bus. Just watch the back. There's a hole in the floor over the exhaust."

"Just like the Lady Line," I muttered, as I climbed into the bus.

Sam closed the hood, picked up his book and hopped into the driver's seat.

"All aboard?" he called.

"Yeah. That would be me," I replied.

"Just checking."

We played license plate games for most of our trip, stopping only to eat canned food that Sam heated over the engine. I tried to get some sleep, but the combination of expired corned beef hash and poor shock absorbers made me quite uncomfortable. It was early morning when Sam finally slowed the bus down at my destination. "Here ya go," he said, as the bus pulled up in front of a small set of stores.

"This is it?" I asked.

"Yup," he replied. "Erasmus."

"Hey, Sam, can you give me a minute to change into my suit?"

"Sure, kid. I'm going to go heat up another can of that corned beef hash. I've been hankering for that for a while. Want some?"

"No thanks."

I reached into my backpack and pulled out a somewhat gnarled suit. I lifted it up, brushed a few spots off it, and decided it would do. The smell of hot hash greeted me as I exited the bus. Sam slammed the hood and walked back with a bowl of food in his hand.

"Well, here I go," I said. I picked up my backpack and waved as he started to close the door, then turned back and asked, "Hey, you come back here?"

"Sure. A bus comes through daily. Noon. High noon."

"Good to know. Thanks, Sam."

"Sure kid. Good luck!" The bus door closed behind me, and Sam headed out onto the road, leaving in his wake a trail of dust and small engine parts.

I eyed my surroundings. The long bus ride, dusty wake of the bus, and corned beef hash had left an unpleasant taste in my mouth. It was then I spotted Agnes's Convenient and went looking for a mint.

Chapter Four
Mrs. Davenport

Things were turning out much differently than I had expected. Upon arrival in Erasmus I had been proclaimed a prophet and handpicked by the Angel of Death to save the town. Perhaps the long rough ride had played tricks with my mind.

I looked over the directions I'd gotten from Mrs. Davenport. Route 35 became Main Street. Make a right at the First Erasmus Bank of Merit. Turn left onto Calendula Street. Come in the back door if your shoes are dirty. The last item was underlined. It was probably better to get lost than have dirty shoes, but considering the size of Erasmus, getting lost would be next to impossible. I began walking.

Outside my destination, I eyed my reflection in the window of a parked car, straightened my tie and brushed a hand across my hair. Careless hair, that's what my particular hairstyle had been called in a popular song. But not everyone appreciates careless hair. Today was probably not the best day for my hair to seek its own pattern of expression.

I checked my breath, a reassuring mix of bleach and peppermint, fine as long as I didn't have to kiss anyone. From what I knew of Mrs. Davenport, I figured I didn't have to worry. I checked to see that the previous morning's shave was still holding up. I carry a portable razor, just in case. I wanted to look as good as possible for Mrs. Davenport. I had the feeling that disapproval was rather commonplace for her.

Glancing down at my shoes, I scuffed a locust body off the top and checked the soles for muck. How much was too much? Normal existence on this planet means a certain quantity of debris will be carried along on one's footwear. Mrs. Davenport was clearly fastidious, however. *Best to play it safe and enter via the back door,* I thought.

I surveyed the building, an old Victorian home now housing offices. There was a large sign out front that read "Davenport Enterprises." Listed underneath were various businesses that fell under the Davenport corporate umbrella. The First Erasmus Bank of Merit. Quik Clean Laundromat. Agnes's Convenient. Deep and Grubby Floor Mats.

Betty's House of Beauty. Veronica's Cheerleading School. Zuzu's Petals Flower Shop. No Name Auto.

Underneath the list of names was the line "Proprietors of every business in Erasmus," written in boldface type. The disclaimer "*Except the Instant Coffee Cup" followed this statement. In smaller print still there was the caveat, "But we'll own them soon."

I walked over to a small white gate fronting a walkway that led to what appeared to be the back door. The walkway was lined with parallel rows of white fence that formed a barricade on either side of the path all the way to the door. On the gate a sign that read "$1.00 Entrance Fee" was positioned above a coin slot and a tray for bills. There was also a slot for credit or ATM cards.

Briefly I considered jumping the gate, but quickly realized it would be embarrassing to spend my first day in Erasmus debating the situation with toll authorities. Hey, when in Rome do as the Romans do. Of course, that policy hadn't worked well for the early Christians, who tended to find themselves introduced to hungry lions.

I decided to go the paper money route. I reached into my pocket, found a crisp one-dollar bill, and slid it into the bill tray, only to have it returned. After un-creasing a corner, I reinserted it and green lights above the tray flashed as the gate swung open.

I walked the narrow fenced-in path to the back door. Three steps led up to the door itself. That Mrs. Davenport was not only the owner of Deep and Grubby Floor Mats but also one of its biggest customers was evident from the steps. The first stair had a welcome mat that read, "Did you wipe your feet?" "Do you really think that's good enough?" questioned the second. The mat on the third step demanded, "C'mon, whom do you think you're fooling?" I scraped my shoes so hard I thought the soles might actually wear off. I felt all the anxiety of child who had been sent to the principal's office.

The door itself was distinctive. I rang the doorbell and waited. An initial blurry movement became an eyeball peering at me through the peephole. It surveyed me for a moment before the doorknob turned and the door opened, revealing a diminutive woman.

"Hello," she said.

"Hello. I'm Andrew Benoit." I extended my hand but none appeared in response. I pulled my hand back to my side in subtle embarrassment. I wondered if they shook hands in Erasmus or if that social practice had not reached it yet.

"Yes, you are."

"Nice door," I stammered nervously.

"It's Wittenberg Wood," she exclaimed. "Of course." Despite her size Mrs. Davenport's presence filled the doorway. She eyed me uncertainly. I almost expected her to dab a small cloth to her tongue, reach over and wipe a smudge from my face. Her dress was immaculate and cut to the contours of her body. Her hair was creatively coiffed. Her skin looked freshly exfoliated. The morning sun reflected off her large diamond ring and hit me directly in the right eye. I reeled in painful response and squinted to protect my eyesight.

She was a good eight inches shorter than my six-foot frame but managed to convey the impression she was looking down over her glasses at me. This was even stranger when you consider that she wasn't wearing glasses.

"You may enter," she said.

I followed Mrs. Davenport down a long hallway. On the walls were portraits of famous American men: George Washington, Thomas Jefferson, Andrew Jackson, Ulysses Grant, and finally Benjamin Franklin, arranged in ascending order according to the value of the American currency on which they appeared. It seemed Mrs. Davenport could have given the Pre-Christmas Ebenezer Scrooge a run for his money in terms of golden idols. At the end of the hallway was a large portrait I recognized to be the present Secretary of the Treasury. Across from that was a large unsmiling picture of the Chairman of the Federal Reserve.

Mrs. Davenport ushered me into her office at the end of the hallway, pointing me to a chair facing a large desk covered with papers. "Can I get you some water?"

"Yes, please," I responded. Between the bleach and the road I was parched.

She handed me a foam cup of water. "Well," she said, as she sat down in a big leather chair. "We have quite a bit to discuss, don't we?"

You have no idea, I thought. *I spoke with Death earlier this morning and am seriously considering directing him to this address first.*

"Yes" I replied, looking around the room at artifacts and other objects that I imagined had been collected over the years. On the wall were numerous "Erasmus Businesswoman of the Year" awards, which appeared to have been given by Davenport Enterprises.

"Now," she said, reaching up into the bookcase next to her desk and removing a large notebook, "this is our lectionary." A lectionary is a compilation of suggested readings for weekly sermons.

"You don't use Bartleby's?" I asked. Bartleby's was the most common sermon provider.

"Oh no," she replied. "That doesn't work for us." There was a slight intonation on the word *us*. Bartleby's was widely considered to set the standard for lectionaries, but Mrs. Davenport considered it inadequate.

“Who put this together?” I asked.

“I did,” she responded with a substantial note of pride. “I have been the preacher here for the past ten years.”

I thought back to my conversation with Death earlier this morning. I needed to warn this town somehow. I had been called on to arouse the passions of the people so that they could repent.

“Mrs. Davenport, I need to talk about Death,” I said.

“Oh, of course! There’s nothing like Death to keep people in line. I’m not big on hellfire and brimstone, but feel free to throw that in if it works for you.”

“No,” I stated emphatically. “I need to warn the people of this town right away that Death will come to them if they don’t repent.”

“And even if they do.”

I wasn’t making myself clear. “Mrs. Davenport, the Angel of Death warned me this morning that Erasmus would be destroyed if the citizens didn’t regain their lost faith.”

“The Angel of Death.” She gave me a hard look, then reached up behind her and pulled down a huge binder.

“I’d advise you to look through these. They are very good. I like them very much.” She closed the book with a smack of satisfaction and handed it to me. I glanced quickly at some of the topics. “Why Women and Orphans no longer need help”; “Pull Yourself Up by The Bootstraps”; “Work Hard, It Keeps God Smiling”; and “Armageddon and You.”

I placed the cumbersome volume at my feet. This job was going to be a challenge. I’d questioned my faith thousands of times. Mrs. Davenport suffered no such uncertainty. She believed in something.

“I am a prophet,” I said.

“Not for profit?” Mrs. Davenport replied. “Oh, no, I don’t believe in them at all. A bunch of people seeking handouts.”

Are there no workhouses, are there no prisons? Thank you, Charles. Over a hundred years later and it still works. Sometimes I think the good lines have all been taken.

"Andrew," she said, staring at me. "Do not preach from Exodus. It gives people odd ideas. After all, those Israelites had it pretty good."

Are you thinking of the same Israelites I am, I wondered? The ones who had been enslaved? Whose sons had been killed? Mrs. Davenport certainly had a creative view of the Bible. It was obvious she did not want to hear the cry, "Let my people go," anywhere near her factories. Few welcome mats were made by Israelites wandering the desert.

"I want people to think about what's coming after. Not about what they get now. Immediate gratification, that's all some people want," she said, with a slight air of annoyance.

"Sure," I replied in resignation. This sort of situation hadn't been covered in seminary.

"Now," she said, as she rolled a long piece of paper out onto the desk. "Here is your contract."

I glanced quickly at the paper, which made me yet another employee of Davenport Industries. There was a brief job description with a small note under "Responsibilities" that read "and all other duties as requested by Mrs. Davenport." Oh well.

The way things were shaping up Erasmus was going to be dust by the end of the week. I figured a contract wasn't binding after that.

"Let's get you to the church," she said. She ushered me back down the hallway ahead of her. The two Founding Fathers, Abe, Ben, and Ulysses all had a look of warning about them. The Federal Reserve chairman's eyes appeared to be shut. *They've seen more than they wanted to,* I thought.

We left by the back door, the voluminous notebook clasped under my right arm. I figured the tollgate would be like most bridges, you pay going one direction and the other way is free. I was wrong. The sign on the exiting side said "$2.00 Exit Fee." Mrs. Davenport's eyes were purposely focused elsewhere. I grumbled slightly as I fumbled in my pocket for two one-dollar bills.

Fortunately, the first two were crisp enough. The gate swung open and the green lights flashed. Mrs. Davenport followed rapidly in my footsteps to avoid the closing gate, a small smile on her face. It was the happiest I had seen her.

She pointed to a building next to her office. "That is the First Church of Erasmus." My sense was that it was the only church in Erasmus. That wouldn't exactly constitute false advertising, but I was beginning to think it should be called the First Church of Davenport. I wondered if God actually entered or was denied access due to dirty shoes. There was a large sign in front of the church: "Money is the Root of all Evil—So Give it to Us." Mrs. Davenport gazed at it with pride.

The church was ordinary, simply decorated on the outside with plain windows. I hadn't expected much, and those expectations were confirmed.

"I saved the church when it had no money," Mrs. Davenport told me.

"Funny, I thought it was the other way around. I thought the church saved people," I said.

"Don't be sarcastic!" she replied caustically. It was the first break in composure, and what was revealed was not pleasant.

"This," she said as she swung the wide church door open, "is my church."

The First Church of Erasmus was efficiently arranged. There was a stand at the front from which I would be speaking. Small windows ran the length of the walls and allowed light to penetrate the somewhat musty building. There was stagnancy in the air but I could not determine its source.

"Now," she said. "Listen carefully as I explain my seating system."

Seating system? People come in and sit where they want to in church. That's how it works, except during weddings and funerals.

I looked down at the sides of the pews. There were small nameplates tacked to each one. On the front pew the name Davenport was listed, not surprisingly, on the plate. Underneath was the name Richardson.

"I seat people according to how much money they have in the bank. My bank," she added.

"Like at society fundraisers," I said.

"Yes. A church can't survive without money," she stated with intense indignation. "You do want to get paid?"

"Or like on public television," I continued. I wanted to ask if she gave out toasters or sweatshirts but resisted. Yes, I did want to get paid. I just didn't want to receive my paycheck from Satan.

"It's just the same as business," she informed me acerbically.

I looked down again. Each row had several names listed. It was a simple system: The wealthiest people had the best seats, seats nearest the heat and ergonomically constructed. Mr. Richardson, explained Mrs. Davenport, was president of the bank. Mr. Tappanzee in the second row was vice president. Row by row as I walked toward the back I guessed at the occupations of the people who placed their posteriors in that section. Everyone in town could tell by looking how much money the other residents had. The church was set up as a reward system for those who were affluent.

"Do people ever move up?"

"If they work hard," she replied. "I review periodically the amount everyone has invested in the Treasury of Merit. And of course, some people move back. That's life."

Life was that simple in Erasmus. Enter the world with a silver spoon and most likely you'll find yourself singing in luxury from the front row. Start out poor and you end up watching the backs of heads and struggling to hear the music. I doubted there was even heat in the back. A collection of coin-operated space heaters confirmed my suspicion.

I walked to the last row. The final pew was poorly constructed, with nails sticking out of a rickety bench built of misfit lumber. The name Constantine had been scrawled in pencil on the side.

How long had the Constantines endured their existence at the bottom? Did they hope for someone to fail so they could move just one row up? I knew what it felt like to wait year after year for a God who was supposed to see everyone as equal. As a child I'd had to go through the lost and found at school for clothes because my family couldn't afford them. Once I found a pair of shorts that I really liked, and had walked around the locker room before a soccer game, pleased with my new apparel. When I got out onto the field, Peter Garston, laughing, yelled out, "Hey, those were my shorts!" I left the field in humiliation. The father of another of my friends, Alan Gladstone, once said "Nothing personal" as he took the present I brought for his son's birthday party and shut the door in my face.

Here at the First Church of Erasmus, Mrs. Davenport had reinvented the needle so as to allow for the easy insertion of a camel. Heaven, Erasmus-style, was full of the rich. It was the poor who could not even get through the gates.

"Who are the Constantines?"

"Oh, *them*." Mrs. Davenport cringed as she looked at the last row. "They will never move up in Erasmus. I'm hoping they move away. Out."

Somewhere a phone rang. "Will you excuse me for a moment?" she asked, and bustled off up the aisle. I sat down on the Constantine's hard bench, running a hand over the splintery seat. Just move away? Out? *It's not that simple,* I thought. *You can move to the end of the earth, but you take who you are with you. Distance does not solve the problem. There is no away, Mrs. Davenport. Not even for what you might think of as trash.*

Chapter Five

The Night Sky

We moved a lot when I was a child. My parents, older brother Jamie, and I inhabited structures of every shape and size, mostly crunched apartments in the worst parts of the city. Once we all slept in a single room in a boarding house. For a while we took up residence in a Dodge van. The best place we stayed, though not for long, was a big house on Handy Street. I learned early not to become attached to anything.

The routine was pretty similar each time. I'd be sitting in class at school and called to the front of the room. The teacher would hand me a note. I'd look around at the other students in the classroom, their curiosity piqued, crumple the piece of paper as if it meant nothing, and stuff it into my pocket. I'd read it later when no one was watching.

The note would give me directions on which bus to take to get to my new home. Neighbors and friends had packed my stuff under the watchful eye of whichever irate landlord was evicting us this time. And that night, like every night, I would go to bed praying that for once we would stay put. I never knew when I woke up in the morning what ceiling I would be looking up at that night.

Once I'd come home and found nobody there.

"Mom," I shouted. No answer. I ran upstairs and searched each room. "Mom!" I screamed. "Jamie!" I was surrounded by silence. My mother finally came home, hours later, and found me under a bed sobbing.

Fortunately we stayed in one town so I could attend the same school. But I never really knew what address to give my friends, so I didn't invite them over. Life was just that way in the Benoit family.

The moves were predicated by my father's presence or absence. When he arrived, we moved into something new. His reappearance meant he had gotten a new job, and that meant more money coming in. Whenever he left, we moved back out. It was that simple. I even made up my own saying: "Dad Leaves in the Morning, Andrew Take Warning; Dad Stays at Night, Andrew's Delight."

The house on Handy Street was my favorite. It was a large old Victorian with gables and a long stairway to the second floor. It was big enough for extensive games of hide and seek. It was the only house we ever lived in where I had my own room.

Still, sometimes I would sleep on the floor in Jamie's room, talking and planning the adventures we would have when we got older. Jamie would doze off while I was talking to him. He told me once that when I'd talk at night it was like listening to the gentle tapping of rain on a roof, and in its calming and reassuring way, it would lull him to sleep.

Jamie was my idol. It was that simple. I suppose I put him on a pedestal, but I believed that he deserved it. He always appeared so much more complete than I was, a better athlete, willing to take chances. If he recognized fear, then he also welcomed it as nothing more than a cautionary friend. While I stepped tentatively out into the world, Jamie ran full force into whatever was happening.

When we went swimming at the lake, Jamie would climb up a rickety board ladder to a rope someone had hung from a tree branch, swing out over the lake, flip into the air and dive into the water.

"C'mon, Andrew!" he'd yell from the water.

"You sure it's safe?" I asked. It looked pretty shallow to me. I measured risk by the teaspoonful while Jamie counted in buckets.

"Just do it!"

Finally I ventured out on the rope. "That was great," I said, as I shivered in the water, only partly from the cold.

But Jamie never gave me a hard time about being afraid. Many brothers would have, and in some ways that can be helpful. But Jamie and I knew from an early age that we would need each other to survive in this world.

He was one of the most popular boys. It didn't matter where we moved, Jamie always established himself as a leader. While I cringed in shyness walking into a new classroom, Jamie grew stronger at the thought of adventure.

"Just be friendly with people," he'd say. "It's not easy for me either, I just work hard at it."

He protected me from bullies, and never told my mother. Instead he shared his infectious laugh at home. He would mimic the antics of his favorite TV characters, like Bugs Bunny and the Three Stooges. He'd roll on the floor in hysterics, and I'd laugh because he was laughing.

There was a small hill to one side of the Handy Street house, where Jamie and I would lie on summer days, comparing interpretations of the cloud formations that floated overhead. With our hands under our heads, bottles of soda to drink, and a free afternoon, we were blessed with the grace of each other's company.

"Cow," I'd say.

"Dragon with a large pipe carrying a knapsack full of chocolate," Jamie would respond. He was always more creative. If I thought a cloud looked like a cat or a dog, Jamie could see in the same nebulous form an ancient beast, a hero holding a plate of Chinese food and riding on a sled, or one of his teachers standing at the front of the class telling everyone that they could have recess all day. I saw basic forms. Jamie saw possibilities.

Sometimes we would lie on the hill at night, and my father would join us. My father's religion focused on the sky. He said that God spoke to us through the stars, the wind, and the rain. That way God could communicate with everyone in the same language, he told us.

Father especially loved the stars. He'd once been a sailor, and had used the stars as guides. He believed in the magic they contained. "Look, Andrew," he said, as we lay on our backs looking up at the night sky. "That's Cassiopeia. She was a fortune teller." He told Jamie and me stories to match the different groupings of light.

"What's that one?" Jamie asked. He knew the answer but loved to hear my father talk about it.

"That's the Big Dipper. It's an asterism, part of a whole constellation called the Great Bear. See the very tip of the handle?" he asked, as he pointed up to the sky.

"Yes," we both replied.

"Can you see a few stars there?" he questioned.

"Well. . . ." Jamie and I squinted. I could see two stars at least.

"Those stars were used as an eyesight test years ago. Only people with the best eyesight could see them. Usually," he said, "that was the kids."

"Like us!" shouted Jamie. We giggled. We could both see the stars at the very tip, a huddled group with unclear outlines, but still we could distinguish more than just light.

"The Native Americans thought those stars represented a bear. The stars behind in the handle of the Dipper are the hunters searching for the bear. At first the bear was on the ground."

"What happened?" I asked.

"Well, one of the hunters caught the bear and swung it around by the tail and threw it up into the sky."

Jamie started laughing. Sometimes Jamie would just break out in laughter because he would get an imaginative vision.

"Maybe that bear just ran up there by himself," he said enthusiastically.

"Some people say that," my father replied.

"I'm a bear," Jamie said, pointing at the stars. "I will never let those hunters catch me. I'll take them through thickets and be laughing all the way. They'll never get me!" Jamie was a fast runner and a great athlete, and loved the challenge of the race. He chortled at the thought of the trouble he would cause as the bear, dashing as he did through the park when we lived in the city, running far ahead of me so I would lose sight of him and get scared, only to hear laughter coming from behind some nearby tree where he'd stopped to play a trick on me.

We were a family that belonged in the night sky, moving around now and then, each of us with our own way of dealing with the light we were given. If my brother was a bear, my father was Halley's Comet. When he arrived in town he brought cascades of light with him. He was a tall man with a big, hearty laugh, exciting and full of energy. And if my father were Halley's Comet, my mother was the moon. She never really had her own light; she just reflected that of others, a gentle, soft and effervescent glow. At times she would appear dark and quiet, but when my father was around, she was full.

We had a big living room in the house on Handy Street. My father would move the furniture aside and put an old record on the stereo. "May I have this dance?" he would ask, offering my mother his outstretched hand. They danced around the living room floor while my brother and I watched, cheering them on now and then. My father would tip mother back and then twirl her around, and we would cheer louder than ever. Eventually they would allow us to join in. The record would repeat over and over as we moved around the floor.

But Halley's Comet only comes around now and then, and unlike the comet, my father was not predictable. I spent many childhood nights awake, staring out the window, hoping he'd return.

"What are you, Andrew?" Jamie asked, as we looked up at the night sky.

I searched the constellations and the various stars within them. I wanted to be Halley's Comet, full of dazzle and adventure. I wanted to be another bear in the big dipper, running across the sky with Jamie. Sometimes I even wanted to be the moon, relying on others for illumination, and quietly settling into the sky, but that wasn't me. None of those fit.

"I am the North Star, Polaris," I replied. That was what I was. Stationary. People knew where to look for me. I would be the point that would help to guide the rest of them to safety. That's what I told them. I would be a guide.

"Not all people want to be guided, Andrew. Many do not care to follow," said my father.

"I will make them care," I said.

"But many people do not want to hear the truth."

"Someday they will," I replied.

My father was silent. I suppose he could have warned me, but would I have listened? Perhaps he figured I was right or maybe felt I needed to learn on my own. A father has a duty to allow the child to grow, to find his own path.

"Although . . . what if there is a storm?" I asked, "and nobody can see me?"

"Have you ever heard of St. Elmo's Fire?"

"No."

"It's a blue light that hits the main mast of a ship during a horrible storm."

"It's for the sailors?"

"Yes."

"So a saint guides the sailors through the storm?"

"Yes. Using the light."

"I don't think I could ever be a sailor. I'm afraid of the water."

"We all sail, Andrew," he said. "But in different ways and across different oceans."

The storms came and went in my family. I never saw a blue light or a saint. One morning I awoke earlier than usual, though I was always the first to get up. Jamie could sleep through anything, and my mother was often hung over. I went to the refrigerator to get milk for my cereal and noticed a note. Groggily I took it to my mother, thinking it might be from my father, telling her he needed a ride home from his night job. It was from my father, but that's not what it said.

That's how it ended. With a note. I had been the bearer of the news and always felt somehow responsible. Halley's Comet had left in silence.

My mother pretended that life had not changed. Our father would return, she told us. But the truth was that he had found another solar system in which to orbit. Jamie and I were the only sources of light mother had now, and she focused all of her energy on returning what we gave to her. She found a job and managed to move us to a nice apartment; it was the longest that we would stay in any one dwelling. Ironically, it was also the place that least felt like home.

When my father left, Jamie stopped laughing. It wasn't that he didn't try. He just couldn't. Sometimes he would respond to a joke with what appeared to be a smile or laughter, but I could tell he was faking it. I never heard him laugh sincerely again.

I never told Jamie when, much later, I found my father's death certificate. I decided to keep it a secret. I wanted to talk with him about it, but I was afraid it would hurt him more. Maybe I even believed that one day my father would return. I continued to look out the window for a sign. But before long it was too late; Jamie didn't seem to care.

* * *

"Andrew!"

"Mrs. Davenport!" I looked up. Her diamond connected with a shaft of sunlight gleaming through the church windows. Ouch. And I was cold again, shivering.

"You've been daydreaming, I think. I said your name four times."

I thought about explaining. *But no,* I thought. *Right now I need a church, this church. The rest will have to wait.*

"Can we see my house?" I asked.

Chapter Six

Touring Erasmus

Mrs. Davenport twisted and turned the knob on a door at the opposite end of the church, cursing softly as she struggled, stopping briefly to look over at me with a gritted teeth smile. Finally with a kick and a shove, the door opened and the room sighed a cloud of dust out into the entryway. Immediately Mrs. Davenport ducked deftly as a large harpoon sailed past the crown of her head, grazing her firmly sprayed coiffure, and rammed into the wall behind the altar. A cacophony that sounded like thousands of bottles and cans crashing to the ground followed, and a bucket full of water dropped from a rope. I could see a number of places where the wall surface near the lodged spear had been spackled. Finally a lone soda can rolled out noisily from the open doorway and stopped at Mrs. Davenport's heel. She kicked it out of the way.

"Silly alarm system."

Oddly enough, the harpoon reminded me of my previous concerns about destiny. It appeared I would at least be well protected from whale ingestion and spewing while in my own home. Life provides. Even for a prophet.

"This way." Mrs. Davenport beckoned me to follow her, sweeping a hand in front of her face to protect herself from debris. With a click of her heels she disappeared within.

It was obvious that the pastor's dwelling had not been used in a few years. There were cobwebs in the windows, and a sense of isolation prevailed. Large dust bunnies glowered from beneath the furniture. Note to Saint Teresa of Avila: The place was no interior castle.

"This is the living room," Mrs. Davenport said, pointing out a small area with a brown couch and a coffee table. The walls were paneled. Okay, here's where my finite interior decorating sensibility finds itself crossed. Who thought of paneling? Have they been prosecuted? "Sealing in the seventies" is the way I look at it.

"Is there a washer and dryer?" I asked.

"Yes," she replied. "In the basement."

"Do they work?" Best to check these things. I'm a cautious sort. Sure, I'd seen Death earlier, but like Scrooge I was wondering if that been nothing more than the ill effects of bad digestion, the culprit being old canned hash.

“Of course the house has a working washer and dryer,” she snapped. “And here’s the kitchen.” She pointed to an area with a stove, a sink, and an avocado green refrigerator.

“Do you get cable or Internet access here?” I asked.

Mrs. Davenport shrugged. “We don’t need those in Erasmus. Life is complicated enough.”

“Nobody has Internet access?” I asked, shocked. I prepared to put myself in the Trendelenburg position, bracing myself against a wall and contemplating an empty life. Having no spam or pop-ups was the only redeeming factor.

“The only windows we have are the kind that you look out.” She pointed at the nearest example, stopping for a moment to stare at a pink dogwood in full flower in the meadow beyond. I saw her shoulders drop, and a quiet came over the room. Her ring hand fell to her side, and the diamond appeared dull compared to the bright blossoms.

"Mrs. Davenport?" I moved past my concern about lack of communication with the outside world. Perhaps it's best. I'm tired of seeing life dissected in the news. Life is to be lived, not reported.

"Mrs. Davenport?" I asked again.

She sighed and then morphed quickly back into full reptilian form. "Yes?" There was frost in her words, and I knew the thaw had not been complete.

"Do you have keys to this place?" I asked.

"Yes, yes," she replied, dumping the contents of a small envelope into her hand. "Now, this is the key to the church," she said as she poked a red-tipped key. "And this is the key to the side door." She handed me keys.

"Thank you." The keys were dangling from a Davenport Industries key chain. I looked for a pass card that would allow me free access through the Davenport Industries gate, but none was connected.

"These are not to be duplicated," she said firmly. "And no overnight guests. After all, you are the pastor."

I felt like I had just been given the rules for Mrs. Davenport's Finishing School. Napkin-folding at 5 PM. Watercress sandwich making at 6 PM.

"Mrs. Carstairs will be contacting you about the music," she added. "And let me know about your sermon. If need be, I can always dust off one of my old ones."

"I'll be fine," I replied, with a slight hint of indignation. I was going to have to give a sermon that would cause the congregation of Erasmus to make big changes. If Mrs. Davenport was typical of the other residents, I might as well have been Sisyphus pushing a boulder up the hill. In fact it might as well just roll over me. Please. Do it now.

"Well," she said finally. "You probably want to get moved in. I'm sure you'll want to get cleaned up before the service tomorrow." She looked me up and down pointedly, walked to the side door of the rectory, opened the door, and scuffed her feet on the "In God We Trust" doormat. Deep and Grubby strikes again. "You might want to clean up this mess."

"I'm thinking of using the harpoon in the service," I said. It seemed like a good opportunity.

Harpoons are hard to come by, at least in this part of the country.

"Clean it first. It's dusty." She turned and left. Through the front window I saw her briskly clicking heels heading back to her office. Time is money.

I eyed the Erasmus First Bank of Merit calendar on the wall. The great beauty of Erasmus was advertised. I flipped through the months. No beach and ocean. Cows and soy and barns predominated. *What am I doing here?* I wondered. Why me? *Why do I always end up at the back of the line? The last shall be first. But when might that change take place, and who notifies whom?*

I sat on the soft, brown couch. I had no one to talk to. I don't know how to save a town.

First things first. I unpacked my belongings on the bed, put everything away, and decided it was time to explore the great city of Erasmus. It would be nice to get a cup of coffee and something to eat. Perhaps once I was more settled, the outlook would seem brighter.

On the front steps, in full sunshine, I felt an unexpected surge of enthusiasm and excitement. I took my Cubs hat off my head and threw it up in the air, Mary Tyler Moore-style. It caught in a tree. I decided to wait until they won the World Series to get it down.

My first stop was the Erasmus Historical Society, which shared space with Natty Gann's Bait and Tackle Shop. It was open on alternate Saturdays from two until four o'clock and on something called Erasmus Day. The outside kiosk had a few informational flyers. I took five to build their self-esteem; surely the normal demand was small. I do my bit when I can. Grace comes in small doses.

The town's founder was Erasmus Cotter, a sixteen-year-old adventurer who'd hitched a ride west with the Donner party when, according to his diaries, his poor sense of humor and lack of personal hygiene caused him to be dropped abruptly on the bare space that became this town. It was the first documented case where lack of cleanliness and humor had saved a man. With luck, a few handmade tools, and an oversized abandoned chicken coop, he was able to build himself a house. Eventually he met and married a woman from Oklahoma.

Other families soon followed. The fledgling town was on a busy trade route that led west, and those who got sick and tired of traveling often gave up and put down roots. Children on wagon trains who asked, "Are we there yet?" would be silenced by the threat of a lifetime in Erasmus. Settling here meant never really getting where you were going. The informational brochure painted the picture pretty clearly. Erasmus was not just a bridesmaid and never a bride; it wasn't even invited to the wedding. Still, it had survived while other towns disappeared. Call it good fortune. Call it providence. Luck is most likely.

Erasmus suffered in the late 1960s, when the Interstate that bypassed the town was expanded. Tourists, who had once gotten off at Erasmus for trinkets, fast food, and gas, now found it more convenient to refuel on the Interstate. Sales of "At Least I Got This Tee Shirt Since We Had to Stop at Erasmus" tee shirts and mugs printed with "Erasmus, a good place to drive through," plummeted, and Erasmus struggled again for survival.

Floor mats appear to have been the salvation. The Deep and Grubby Floor Mat Company employed most of the town, and there were also a few other small businesses. It appeared that every citizen was in some way an employee of Davenport Industries. In Davenport, we trust. Or maybe we don't.

I walked down Main Street, past the library and Zuzu's Petals Flower Shop, and up the steps to The Instant Coffee Cup. I love coffee. Good coffee. Fresh ground coffee with cream and sugar. Not two percent milk. Not whole milk. Half and half will do.

This was the only business that did not have a welcome mat produced by Deep and Grubby. A bell rang as I swung the door open. Inside there was a counter with a few rotating stools. On the wall behind the counter was a copy of a Norman Rockwell painting of a police officer sitting next to a boy at a luncheonette counter. Next to the painting, there was a photograph of a real police officer and a child.

"You must be the new pastor," the man behind the counter said as I walked toward him.

"Well, yes, how did you know?" I asked. Had a few angels arrived before me in order to trumpet the arrival of a prophet?

"We all heard you were coming today. I'm John Luther Zwingli," he said, offering his hand to shake. He was a gangly man with the look of one who has lived—or at least thought about it periodically.

"Andrew Benoit." I extended my own hand. "You have an interesting name."

"It's a combination of my mother's and my father's last names. I use both of them. The Zwinglis and the Luthers were in the baking business. My mom was a Zwingli and my dad was a Luther. They met one summer while making croissants. My mother always said she was attracted by my father's buns."

"I suppose that means both of your parents were well bred," I smiled.

"That was half-baked," John replied.

"Sorry."

"Actually I was lucky," said John. "They may not have had lots of dough, at least not the kind that buys bicycles and toys, but we were close. So, what would you like?"

"Cup of coffee."

"What kind?" he asked, pointing to a row of jars. The choices were Folgers, Chock Full of Nuts, Maxwell House, and Peggy's Organic.

"You only have instant?"

"Well, yeah. Hence the name. We live in a drive-through society. Everyone wants it now or earlier. We have instant coffee and non-dairy creamer. We even have instant oatmeal for those who want something substantial to eat. Haven't sold much of that lately, but I will after the weather turns cold."

Sigh. "I'll try the Peggy's Organic," I said. John reached under the counter for a jar, opened it slowly and scooped out a tablespoon. He handed me a foam cup with the dry brown granules in the bottom. "Cream and sugar are behind you, hot water is over there. Make it fresh and to your liking!" If this was a test I was beginning to think I'd fail.

I sat for a short time pretending to drink the mediocre liquid from the synthetic material cup. This gave me a chance to survey the shop. A group of people sat conversing loudly at a long table in the back.

John Luther Zwingli threw his cleaning towel over his shoulder and walked up to my table.

"So why come to Erasmus?" he asked.

"It was my calling." I said.

"You shouldn't have answered. I've been here five years and don't see it getting any better. As you may have noticed, Mrs. Davenport controls everything." He paused. "Well, except me. I bought the Coffee Cup so there would be one place that wasn't part of her corrupt rule. She's tried to shut me down, but I'm pretty persistent. But," he said as he reached down and wiped at a stain on the table, "lately, I'm not sure."

"Do you do a good business?" I asked. I silently hoped he was staying. Even if his taste in coffee was less than admirable, it did not reflect on the man.

"Not bad," he said. "I'm the only game in town, so I do well enough to get by."

Our conversation was interrupted by loud, hysterical laughter from the rear of the coffee shop.

"Who are they?" I asked.

"They call themselves mystics. They say they're on the way to sainthood," he replied.

Mystics? In Erasmus?

"You know," continued John, "they've been asking for you. Seems they've been waiting."

"For me?"

"Well, you're the new pastor, and it's the new pastor they've been looking out for. Why don't I introduce you?"

"Okay," I replied. Leaving my full cup of coffee on the table, I followed John to the rear of the coffee shop, where the odd group greeted me with halted laughter. All heads turned as I walked up to the table.

"It's Andrew, right?" asked John.

"Yes," I replied.

"Harpo, this is Andrew."

A man dressed in a very drab brown and gray outfit stood up and extended his hand. His shirt seemed to be made of coarse, brittle hair. "I'm the spokesperson for the Mystics," he said, as he honked on his horn. The group laughed cautiously. Clearly they'd seen this before.

"Harpo?" I asked. "Harpo . . . Marx?"

"Yes. We've all taken the names of dead comedians. What better way to honor their great ministry?"

The odd little group nodded in agreement. On the table before them was a catalogue advertising quality hair shirts.

"This is Curly," Harpo said, as another man put his hand up.

"Nice to meet you."

"Nyuk, nyuk, nyuk!" he replied. All I could think was, thank God it's not Shemp. I always hated Shemp.

"Here's one I love," Harpo said, pointing to an attractive red-haired woman who was drinking Vita Meta Vegamet.

"Hi," she said. "I'm Lucy." I kissed her hand. Did she know what happened to Little Ricky? Well, this wasn't the real Lucy; maybe she wouldn't care. Actually, I didn't know what happened to Little Ricky, except he wasn't little anymore. Television is not kind to child actors, that's all.

A man next to Lucy drank from her glass. She grabbed it back.

"I'm a baddd boy," the man bleated.

"Lou Costello," Harpo said, "this is Andrew Benoit."

"Who?"

"Who's on first," I replied emphatically. "Feller's pitching, and I'm Andrew Benoit."

"Glad to meet you finally," he said.

"And this is Mae West," Harpo said, as I eyed a slender woman with short brown hair and without the prerequisite curves. Obviously she had applied for poetic license and received it.

"Are you in town for good?" she asked.

"I expect to be here awhile," I told them. "Probably not for good." She smiled.

Many times, I'd stayed up late at night and watched old movies with my father. He liked Charlie Chaplin. I liked Buster Keaton. If I ever became a mystic, I knew what name I'd take.

Each of the mystics I had met so far was dressed in drab clothing. Their shirts looked like steel wool. They drank the instant swill in front of them with an abandon that signified a sense of true self-flagellation. *It's a deep pain they inflic*t, I thought, watching them sip.

Then Harpo pointed to a man wearing a flowery Hawaiian shirt, green bell-bottoms, a bead necklace, and a smiley-face pin. "This is John Wayne."

"But. . . ."

"We know," Harpo interrupted.

The star of *The Green Berets* and *True Grit* had never been one for pratfalls and guffaws. Though now that I thought about it, some of his less than stellar accomplishments had been known to provoke laughter. I mentioned this to Harpo.

"Go ahead, tell him that," Harpo challenged.

I decided against this, not surprisingly. "Why is he wearing those odd clothes?" I asked.

"Well," Harpo said, "we're ascetics. You can see that most of us are dressed simply."

I nodded.

"Take a look at this," Harpo said, tugging up the top of his undershirt with a tone of pride.

"What is it?" I asked.

"Pure Don King," he said, referring to the lining of his undergarment. "I got it from his barber. Cost me a lot, but it was worth it."

"A hair shirt."

"Right. It itches a lot." He seemed almost boastful.

"So why does John Wayne wear those clothes and not something like this?" I questioned.

"He's doing it his way. Who suffers more than a man wearing a Hawaiian shirt and a smiley-face button?"

He had a point. People who dress differently get singled out. Mrs. Scarpelleti, who lived a few doors down on Handy Street, had always worn a skirt that must have been rescued from the square dance lost and found. Now I wondered if she was a mystic.

Suddenly I felt an odd, cold sensation in my spine. The air seemed to be swirling with frost.

"Get down, Andrew!" John Luther Zwingli shouted. There was a rush of movement at the table.

I dropped to the floor and crouched among the legs of the mystics. Above me the group started an intense discussion about Golden Age comedy, rambling nervously as they strained to maintain the appearance of a calm, normal conversation. Glancing up at the window, I saw the carefully coiffed head of Mrs. Davenport peering into the

Instant Coffee Cup. Her eyes were fixed on the mystics with laser intensity. Finally, she turned away, and the chilly wind departed with her.

"Thank God," Costello said. "Andrew, you can get up now."

"You would have never heard the end of it if you were found in here," John told me. "She hates this place."

"Why?" I asked, pulling myself to a standing position.

"This is one place in Erasmus where she has no influence," he said. "And the one place where God does."

"What do you mean?"

"We have a church service here every morning and also on Friday nights. You're welcome to join us. But you can never tell anyone."

"I won't tell anyone."

"You'll join us?"

"Well, maybe." I looked down at my watch. I had spent most of my afternoon looking around Erasmus. The sun was starting to set, and I had a sermon to write.

"I have to go," I said, and waved to the mystics.

"Goodbye, Andrew!" they called.

"Later, porcupine!" Curly shouted.

"Come back and see me sometime!" exclaimed Mae West.

John Luther Zwingli walked me to the door. "I'm sure you have lots of questions. Come see us again, Andrew."

"Yes," I said. "I will."

Outside the Instant Coffee Cup the coast appeared to be clear. No sign of Mrs. Davenport. Perhaps she was busy handing out eviction notices to women and orphans or engaging in some other devious preparation for power.

I really needed a good cup of coffee. Fortunately, I had brought with me a month's supply of Oscar's Organic Free Range Coffee. Oscar's beans were shade grown and talked to every day by a caring and nurturing mendicant of The Order of Java, a rather nondescript group of spiritual aspirants devoted to their task. Growing coffee required diligence and a higher call. There are lesser forms of commitment. These aspirants were engaged in a noble effort to provide true sustenance to the world. I might save Erasmus, but without good coffee, they would still be lost.

I stopped at the Country Cupboard, a small convenient store like Agnes's, for cream. Unlike Agnes's it was open. The cashier was a short woman wearing a "Beef and Bowl" tee shirt.

"You're the new pastor," she said.

"Yes." I nodded toward her shirt. "So, you like to bowl?"

"No," she replied. "I go there for the beef. It's the best restaurant in town."

If Beef and Bowl set the standard for restaurants I'd probably be wise to forgo any hope of Thai or Indian. I wanted to ask what the locals thought was the worst restaurant in Erasmus, but I figured it was probably the Beef and Bowl.

"That's a dollar fifty-seven," she said.

I reached into my pocket and pulled out a dollar bill, some change and a mint. "Do you run the convenient just outside of town?" I asked, picking out the mint and a piece of lint.

The woman cringed and with a finger beckoned me closer. “That’s run by Agnes,” she whispered.

“Well, it’s never open.”

She glanced quickly around the empty store. “Don’t tell anyone you heard this here,” she said, “but Agnes isn’t coming back. That store will never open again. Someone goes in and cleans and makes the place look presentable, and Mrs. Davenport forces us to take any inventory that might expire.”

“Why?”

“Mrs. Davenport wants to keep it running.”

“Tax write-off?”

“No, not at all,” she said. “She does it for Agnes. Her daughter.”

Agnes was Mrs. Davenport’s daughter? Where was she? Off seeking her fortune in another country? Married to the owner of a rival welcome mat company? Had I met her somewhere and not even known it? Did her store sell those raspberry and coconut covered cupcakes? I only wondered because they are hard to find. Anyway, questions about Agnes would have to wait, because a bell jingled, and the cashier and I both looked around at the door.

"Mrs. Carstairs, how are you?" called the cashier.

"Fine, and you?" asked the rather portly Mrs. Carstairs.

"Fine."

I stepped forward. "Hello. I'm Andrew Benoit, the new pastor." Mrs. Carstairs shook my hand with a surprisingly light touch. I'd been imagining powerful melodies filling the air in the church, providing background for my rousing sermons. *Perhaps,* I thought, *she just takes pains not to injure the delicate fingers of the church pianist.* "Mrs. Davenport told me that you are interested in talking about the music for tomorrow's worship."

"Well . . . yes," she said, with a girlish giggle. "But, she did *tell* you, didn't she?"

"Tell me what?" I asked.

"I only know one song."

Oh. "What song is that?" I asked.

"Amazing Grace. I play it at the beginning and the end of every service."

Amazing, I thought. *It must take a lot of grace for the parishioners to put up with that every week.*

"Well, that will work," I told her. Anything will work when you plan to talk about Death and lamentation. Amazing Grace might be perfect. Twice was a bit much, but who knew, maybe the sound would be sweeter. If nothing else, my brief stay in Erasmus was going to be interesting. I excused myself, picked up my cream, and headed off to write a sermon.

Chapter Seven

Sermon on Amount

I settled onto the large brown sofa with a cup of freshly brewed Oscar's Organic, a Bible, a pen, and a notebook. How does a prophet prophesy? The Bible offers few clues about actual do's and don'ts. I stared at the paneling, the shag carpet. Death had informed me of my official status and my mission. But what should I say? "Get out now!" was a bit like yelling "Fire!" in a crowded movie theater. You create panic, no one knows where to go, and you wind up doing more harm than good. "You are all going to die!" was even worse. Besides, other than Mrs. Davenport, Erasmus didn't seem much wickeder than other towns I knew. I hadn't noticed behavior that warranted destruction. Still, Death had told me the decree. I was just a messenger.

The book of Jonah seemed to provide the best example. Jonah went reluctantly to Nineveh to proclaim its fate. He was pretty determined that the people suffer, but I didn't share that goal. Sure, I would like to watch as Mrs. Davenport repaid all her misbegotten money. Perhaps God could make her liquidate her assets by continually having to enter and exit that awful gate to her house.

I needed to concentrate. It had been a long day. I lay back on the sofa, closed my eyes, and tried to imagine a sermon that would make a whole town repent.

Soon I found myself being drawn toward a light at the far end of a tunnel, where I could see a shadowy figure. Could this be an angel with a message? Was it a prophet? Jeremiah? Ezekiel? Deborah? Elijah? Or maybe even one of my relatives, reaching for me from the other side?

The mysterious creature moved toward me. As it got nearer I realized, with some surprise, that it was hopping on all fours.

"Hey there," it said.

"You . . ." I hesitated. But there was really no question as to his identity. "You are the Velveteen Rabbit."

"Got it in one," the rabbit replied.

Okay, I am a patient sort. But others see heavenly visions like angels, deities, and seraphim, and I get a rabbit filled with fluff. In the midst of a crisis of faith I was sent a stuffed bunny.

"Rabbits don't talk," I said indignantly.

"And the Angel of Death doesn't appear out of washing machines." Snarky. Rabbits are generally regarded as mild mannered. This one was not. Fame must have gone to his head. "Besides, if you can have the gift of prophecy, I can have the gift of speech," he told me.

Touché. I reminded myself to suspend disbelief, just as Jimmy Stewart did in *Harvey*. I'd have preferred Clarence from *It's a Wonderful Life* to a rabbit, though. At least he got his wings.

"What do you want from me?" I asked.

"Nothing. I am here to give you support," the rabbit replied, ruffling his brown fur with the touch of a paw.

"Can you write a sermon?" I asked.

"Hardly. I'm a stuffed animal."

Cheeky little beast.

"You have a difficult task ahead of you. You must not give in," the rabbit continued. "Remember, you have a responsibility to the people of Erasmus."

"How can I make them listen?"

"You must become real first."

"I am real," I said.

"No, Andrew," he replied. "There will be no need to say it once you are."

"I am real!" I shouted. "You're the imaginary one!"

The Velveteen Rabbit hopped back into the shadows, but his words echoed in my head: Remember, you have a responsibility to the people of Erasmus. But to save them you must become real.

I tossed and turned myself awake, shrugging off the last vestiges of sleep. I made some fresh coffee, extra strong, and determined I would write as I had never written before. Well, except once, in defense of a list of parking tickets I had accumulated, but this was more urgent. It was time to think of something that would stir the hearts of Erasmus.

Late into the night, I filled the pages of my notebook with metaphors, similes, synonyms, antonyms, anecdotes, and homilies. I was sure I'd hit just the right note, the one that would reach deep into the souls of every Erasmusian and convince them to repent. Finally I fell asleep at the kitchen table.

The next day, I shaved carefully, dressed in my black suit, and even combed my usually careless hair. This was not a day for carelessness.

At the church, I rehearsed the sermon several times. I stood at the pulpit and looked out at the imaginary crowd, smiling as I pretended they were walking in, imagining the chords of Amazing Grace filling the church and Mrs. Carstairs with a paper diagram pasted over the keyboard so that she could easily find the necessary keys. Maybe the consistency of the music would serve as ritual and outweigh the agony of hearing the same thing over and over. If Mrs. Carstairs suddenly started playing "Rock of Ages," the congregation might think she'd found God but more likely a bottle of something intoxicating.

I looked out over the empty pews. I felt confident in my mind, but my heart was feeling something different. I was going to have to allow God to speak through me and wasn't certain how.

"Good Morning, Andrew!" trilled Mrs. Carstairs.

"Good Morning, Mrs. Carstairs," I replied. "Do you have today's music?" I asked with a tinge of sarcasm.

"I think I'll play Amazing Grace." She laughed a bit.

Suddenly that icy cold feeling in my spine returned, as if someone had dropped an icicle into it.

"Good morning, Mrs. Davenport," I said, turning to her.

"Yes. Now about that sermon."

The chill in my spine traveled throughout my whole body. The only place it could not touch was my stomach, which was in the throes of sudden volcanic indigestion.

"I'm all ready," I said. "A big thank you to Mrs. Carstairs here." Mrs. Carstairs giggled as if she was in fifth grade and one of the boys in her class had just handed her a Valentine.

"Well," said Mrs. Davenport, as she handed me a thick document, "here is one of mine, just in case."

A "just in case" sermon? My mother sometimes sent Jamie and me to school with what she called “just in case” money. Just in case the bullies got your milk money. Just in case you needed to call home in an emergency. Just in case you were walking by Downtown Pastry and had to have a fluffy donut. I had never heard of having an extra sermon.

I glanced at the title. *Banking on God.* Enough said. The Angel of Death was tracking Erasmus for demolition, and the last words of advice from the pulpit would be about starting checking accounts. I stuffed her sermon under my own and prepared to start the service.

The people of Erasmus walked into the church in a pattern that was no doubt ingrained on their souls. They knew their pews by heart. I would guess no one had really moved much in years. Perhaps you could marry into a better pew but that would require leaving your family behind.

Mrs. Davenport greeted the people in the front pews. She glanced toward the back of the church in annoyance as a woman walked quietly in the door, herding her flock of boys into the back row. There was a variance in height, but otherwise they looked very similar, like nesting dolls, each with crewcut hair and a neat white shirt tucked somewhat successfully into his pants. The woman sat between the youngest and the middle boy. It was clear she had a plan and was going to stick to it.

The Constantines, I thought. I watched as the youngest tapped his eldest brother on the head and then turned away, pretending that nothing had happened. The tapping continued until the bigger boy turned and gave the smaller one a tender knock on the skull. The younger boy exploded into tears, and Mrs. Constantine turned to admonish the older child. One of the consistencies of the world will always be the child who starts the trouble and manages to get someone else scolded for it.

The crowd settled. I had the dubious privilege of sitting in the front pew between Mrs. Davenport and Mr. Richardson. Although it was May, I was experiencing an invincible winter, with apologies to Albert Camus. Maybe he'd met Mrs. Davenport. Maybe that's why he didn't believe in God.

She stood. "Good morning," she said, her practiced smile breaking through the lacquered veneer of her skin. "I would like to introduce our temporary pastor, Andrew Benoit." She emphasized the word *temporary*.

Little do you know, Davenport, I thought as I walked to the pulpit. *Unless my sermon works, this is a temporary town.*

I'll admit I was a little nervous. It's not easy to get up in front of a crowd and speak even under the most ordinary conditions. These conditions were anything but ordinary.

"Good morning," I said. "Thank you for welcoming me into Erasmus." I looked out over the crowd, which appeared no different from any congregation you might see in any church: fathers and mothers and children. The mystics and John Luther Zwingli were notably absent. In the back row the Constantine boys were squirming in their seats, and Mrs. Constantine was busy unwrapping candy to quiet them.

It occurred to me that this audience was probably not going to be receptive. Mrs. Davenport wanted profit, not a prophet, and the citizens, it seemed to me, were in the habit of following their shepherdess's lead. I took a deep breath.

"A reading from Jonah." Out of the corner of my eye, I noticed Mrs. Davenport gesturing at me.

"Hair, hair, tie, tie," she mouthed as her hand touched her hair. I feigned a feeble response and moved on.

"Now, we all know this was more than a fish story." I'd decided to start with humor. Humor opens the heart, enables it to listen. I looked out over the congregation, which collectively had the look of an audience watching the Grass Growing channel on cable TV. That old whale option was beginning to look good. OK, forget humor. It wasn't going to work.

"Nineveh is not the only town that displeased God," I told them in a serious voice. "Yesterday I was visited by the Angel of Death. He told me that unless there was repentance in this town, Erasmus would be destroyed by the end of the week."

Mrs. Davenport was motioning much less subtly now. She pointed at her sermon, still lying on the podium. The crowd remained unmoved.

“Death told me that the town of Erasmus has lost its faith. Death told me that I am a prophet. I have come here to warn you. You need to repent.” I was about to repeat the call to repent when Mrs. Davenport drew her flat hand across the front of her neck, and the sound system went dead. She had passed judgment.

“And now,” she said, standing and addressing the crowd, “let’s all sing Amazing Grace.”

Mrs. Carstairs shrugged at me in resignation.

“No, no,” I pleaded loudly. “You must listen!”

It was too late. The sweet sounds of grace had filled the church. My sermon hadn’t even gotten off the ground. The sheep would follow the shepherdess to slaughter. Church was going to be over early today. At least the Constantine boys would be happy.

Members of the church came up and thanked me. “Good sermon,” one man said. “Just about the right length.”

“Next time try Obadiah,” a woman stated. “I love the book of Obadiah.”

"I liked your choice of music."

"You don't understand," I kept telling them. But my words were useless in the void of Erasmus. Long ago, it seems, the words they heard in church had stopped living inside them. Perhaps they had decided it was easier just to pretend interest. After all, interest was what Mrs. Davenport desired.

I am not a real prophet, I thought. *I am a false one*. I'd let my opportunity pass me by.

"Excuse me." Mrs. Constantine was looking up at me. I looked in her eyes. They were tired. Her dress was plain green and it had been washed often. She had a worker's hands.

"Yes?" I asked.

"Pardon me for a moment. . . . Boys!" she said, her voice directed at the three closely cropped heads standing behind her. "Go stand over there." She gestured at the doorway. "And be good!" she emphasized. The boys followed her direction, discretely poking and prodding each other as they moved. You could tell it was only a matter of time before one of them detonated. Mrs. Constantine knew this and spoke efficiently.

"I know you're new," she said. "But I need your help."

"What can I do?" I asked.

"It's Jimmy," she said softly. "My middle boy. He's having trouble in school. Ever since we moved here he has struggled."

"What does he struggle with?" I asked.

"He won't say what's wrong. Jimmy doesn't complain. Never did. That's what worries me about him. I know he's having a hard time with kids at school. His older brother, Jared, punches anyone who bothers him. His younger brother, Peter, seems to fit in very well. But not Jimmy."

"If he isn't complaining, how do you know?" I questioned.

"I hear things. People in town tell me. A woman I work with at the Deep and Grubby told me that her son thinks Jimmy is odd. Jared told me that Jimmy always eats lunch alone. . ." She paused. "I really am worried."

"OK," I said, as Mrs. Davenport's signature chill flooded every orifice of my body.

"Please talk to him," Mrs. Constantine implored quickly, and then walked away.

"Andrew." The cold prong of a hand tapped my shoulder. A storm had begun brewing inside me. The combined clouds of frustration, anger, resentment, and powerlessness were about to connect for what I figured would be a tsunami. I turned to face my adversary.

"You'll have to work on your sermons," she said. "Or better yet use one of mine. Yours was embarrassing. I just couldn't put you or the congregation . . . or me . . . through it."

I wanted to tell her she was wrong but years earlier had developed the habit of squelching my feelings. With Mrs. Davenport, I felt again like a nine-year-old boy standing on the porch of the Gladstones' house, staring at a front door that had just been shut in my face.

"What did Mrs. Constantine want?" she demanded.

"Oh, something about one of her boys."

"She shouldn't have had all those children . . .

The storm of anger began growing in me again.

". . . but I can't control everything."

"No," I snapped. "You can't."

"Remember to allocate your time according to what people are worth," she continued. "Mr. Richardson deserves at least an hour a week. The same for Mrs. Tappanzee."

"And the Constantines?" I asked.

"About a minute," she replied. "If that."

Scrooge had nothing on Mrs. Davenport. In fact, in a contest, he'd take the Congeniality Award. No question.

I stomped away. *I have failed,* I thought. My sermon was awful—the town didn't even respond. I'd had my chance and fallen short. The town of Erasmus would be destroyed, and I was to blame.

I picked up my sermon and my Bible and headed into my house, ignoring the group of people who had amassed for coffee hour. Even if the coffee had been freshly brewed, I wouldn't have been interested. I needed some time alone. I'd never given up on anything in my life, but I was beginning to think I had no choice this time. I felt exhausted and belittled; I'd never felt so defeated.

"God, why did you bring me here?" I asked aloud. I shouldn't really be in Erasmus anyway.

Professor Anderson had talked me into it. How could I have been so stupid?

I'd gotten precisely one hour of sleep the night before, and that was at the kitchen table. I had undressed and climbed onto my lumpy bed. Finding I couldn't sleep, I got onto the floor and climbed under my bed. At least if Death came looking, he would have difficulty finding me. "Should I stay in Erasmus?" I asked over and over as I drifted off. "Should I stay or should I go?"

I dropped into the deep hole of sleep. Perhaps, as the Aborigines said, the real world was just a dream. Had I had selected a nightmare? My consciousness drifted in and out. Figures came and went in my mind. I saw my father, my uncle Andrew, Mrs. Davenport, the Constantines, and my brother Jamie. I tossed and turned on the hard floor.

A familiar figure hopped toward me in my dream. Some say that we are given animal guides or totems. Mine was an internationally famous stuffed bunny, but this time, he looked horrible. His fur was sparse and there were bald patches. He limped. His ears were missing pieces, and one eye was partially detached.

"You look awful," I said. What a mess. His fur looked like the floor mat in a locker room after a rugby game played in the rain.

"I am becoming real," he replied.

That kind of real I don't need, I thought. "Who told you that you are becoming real?" I asked.

"The skin horse," he answered.

"The skin horse? What would a skin horse know?"

"That I am becoming real," the rabbit said again.

I sighed. "I need your help," I said.

"I know."

"Can we do a bit better than that horse?"

The rabbit frowned at me. "I've brought you some help," he said with exaggerated patience. I turned and saw a curtain. The rabbit pulled the curtain open and revealed a set of bleachers with a group of men sitting on the seats. They looked very familiar. Television fathers, that was it.

"Hello, Andrew," they said.

"Hello," I said. "Hey, Mr. Cleaver, how's the Beav?" I'd always wanted to ask that.

"What about me?" demanded Father Mulcahey. "No one ever asks about me."

"Me neither," whined Homer Simpson. "It's always Beav, Beav, Beav."

"Oops," said the rabbit. He pulled the curtain shut and opened another.

"You know, your great-uncle Andrew was quite a pastor," said my father.

"Dad?"

"He traveled all over the world. Come and look." He patted the seat next to him. I sat. "Here he is in Lithuania," he said, pointing to a photo in an album on his lap. "And here's one of him starting a church in Appalachia." The picture showed a man standing in front of a newly constructed church. I remembered having this conversation with my father as a boy, but I'd forgotten it long ago.

"I was named for him?" I asked, just as I had then.

"Yes," my father replied. "He was my father's older brother. He died right before you were born. He was a great man, and you will be, too."

Ha, I thought. *Little do you know.*

"What happened to him?" I asked. "Did he have a family? Do I have relatives I've never met?"

"No, he never married," my father said. "He felt that as he did God's work, the world became his family."

"Why haven't I heard this before?"

"Well," my father paused. "He had been working for a long time with one church. The parishioners loved him, and he gave all of his time to them. Somehow, though, it didn't work out the way he expected. He ended up getting frustrated."

"Why?" I asked.

"He felt that no one was listening. He would hear the stories of unwanted pregnancies, drug and alcohol abuse, and murders in the community. He had given his whole life to God, and this was the result. His parishioners gave lip service but that was it. Eventually, he gave up."

"Oh," I said.

"You see, he wanted to save them but couldn't."

My father had gotten quiet. He waited a moment to speak again. "The last time I visited him he was in the hospital. He looked awful. He'd become so bitter. The resentment had built in him and he could no longer move. It was as if it had taken over his body. He could barely move his lips to speak."

It was hard to reconcile this image with the handsome man in the album, smiling broadly, clearly happy. He had one arm outstretched and was pointing to the structure he had just helped to build.

"I won't get bitter," I promised. "I won't give up."

My father closed the photo album and handed it to me.

"I hope not, Andrew," he said. "Be true to your word."

I glanced down at the album, and when I looked up again, my father was gone and the Velveteen Rabbit was pawing the curtain impatiently. "Goodbye, Andrew," he said. He turned and hobbled off, leaving a trail of mud and lost fur in his wake. Reality was killing him. Faking it was doing the same to me.

A buzzer was ringing in my head. It wouldn't stop. Suddenly, with a startled leap into consciousness, I realized it was my doorbell. I tried to get up from my bed, forgetting I was under it, and smashed my forehead against the wooden slats supporting the box spring.

"Ouch!"

The doorbell rang again, and someone called my name from outside. I rolled out from under the bed and grabbed a pair of jeans and a tee shirt. The bell continued ringing loudly as I made my way downstairs.

"Coming!" The ringing didn't stop. I opened the door and saw through the darkness a small, bald-headed man with his finger attached to my doorbell.

"Andrew Benoit?" he shouted over the bell.

I looked at his finger. "Oh!" He removed it. "Sorry. Guess I just liked to hear the sound of a bell ringing."

"I'm Andrew Benoit."

"Ah, very good," he replied. "Mrs. Davenport would like to see you."

"Now?

"Yes," he said. "At the Deep and Grubby. D and G we call it."

"What time is it?" I felt disoriented by my dreams. How long had I slept under the bed?

"Early. She wants to see you before we open."

"Who are you?"

"Oh, sorry about that. Horace P. Bogardus. I'm Mrs. Davenport's Chief Operations Officer. The COO."

"Right," I said. "OK, Horace, lead me to the lion's den."

I followed him as he ambled up to the tollgate at Davenport Industries. Horace swiped a small card in the machine and the green light went on. He looked back at me and I showed him my empty hands. He nodded and swiped the card again. "C'mon, kid, this one's on me."

"Thanks."

"Just don't mention it to Mrs. D."

"Don't worry."

Horace walked up to the side of the Deep and Grubby Floor Mat Company, checked his hands and wiped them on the sides of his pants before opening the door. "This way," he said. We walked some steps and onto a catwalk that looked out over the factory floor. The factory was dark. Only thin slivers of morning light entered through the windows. Mrs. Davenport stood, perched over the railing. Cold air enveloped a crosswalk beside a large sign that read:

Deep and Grubby Floor Mats
Are Really, Really Swell
If You Do Not Buy Them
You'll Probably Go To _______

"Morning, Mrs. Davenport!" called Horace. He had dropped the informal "Mrs. D."

"Good morning, Horace. Ah, Andrew, I see you need another suit."

"Good morning," I said. "Nice ad."

"Yes, it's very useful. You just fill in the name of a competitor. I thought of it myself. Now, about your sermon."

What sermon? I wanted to ask. You cut me off. I could feel the words in my throat but could not say them.

"I think it's important that you know a bit more about Erasmus. After that sermon yesterday about which, by the way, I got several complaints, I told the people you were nervous and new but that excuse won't last, now will it?"

I could feel my teeth grinding in the back of my mouth.

"I wasn't always rich, Andrew. I had to work to get where I am. When I arrived in Erasmus, I was penniless, a single mother, and I had very little job experience."

"Why come here?"

"I ran out of bus fare."

"Oh," I said.

"I started at Deep and Grubby when it was only the Grubby Company. Albert Grubby owned it. Not a very good businessman. I suppose he was nice, but nice doesn't pay the bills, now does it?"

"Never has for me," I replied. Actually, not spending helped me pay my bills.

"Right. Work pays the bills. I worked hard. I moved up quickly and eventually bought the company. I added the Deep to the name. Everyone wants to be deep these days, don't you think?"

“Sure,” I replied. Deep asleep.

“Andrew, when I got to this town, the entire place was in the throes of a financial nightmare. I turned things around and eventually was able to save Erasmus.”

“That must have been tough,” I said. “You must have had great faith.” I remember when my mother lost her job. Jamie and I were pretty young, but we could tell she was scared. She told us that God tests us and we must keep our faith, or God couldn’t reach us. But every night, I would walk past her room and hear her crying.

“Faith?” Mrs. Davenport replied. “Faith is for children waiting at Christmas for a present. Work is for adults.”

“You worked hard.”

“Yes, and now I employ almost everyone in Erasmus. They are my sheep. I tend to them, feed them, and ask little in return.”

“If one went missing, would you go looking for it?”

“Of course,” she said.

I felt I was experiencing a softer side of Mrs. Davenport. She saw herself as caring for her employees, a shepherdess overseeing the well-being of her flock.

"I would have to find them, to fire them."

Oh.

"It's easier to do when they're outside the building."

"Right."

"Anyway, I brought you here to show you my system. It's quite ingenious. Someday, I'd like to write a book about it. Horace!" she shouted.

Light illuminated the Deep and Grubby factory floor. I could see floor mats laid out, and each one had a number or a letter. Letters across the horizontal spelled Deep and Grubby Floor Mat. The numbers were in order from one to eight and lined the vertical.

"Now mind you, it's not entirely my own invention. I borrowed from . . ."

"Bingo," I said.

"Exactly! Everyone knows Bingo, so it doesn't take much to explain. Now let me show you how it works." I followed her to a large clear vat of balls. The balls had numbers and letters on them that appeared to correspond with those on the mats.

Mrs. Davenport turned a switch, and the balls start gyrating on an air current. One rose up to the top and emerged from the hole, finally settling in a small bowl at the peak of the machine.

"B9," she stated. "I love that employee. Never any trouble."

"I don't get it."

"But they do. Get a break, that is."

"You mean that when you call their number and letter they get to take a break from work?"

"Well, I only do the calling on special occasions. But yes."

"That seems unfair."

"It's perfectly fair. They all get a break and no one gets more than anyone else. The timing may be random, but it's fair. Like life."

"But what if someone needs a break when their number is not lit?"

"They learn to wait. They learn patience. We call the next number when the last person is back. Oh, I love it!" she said, as she watched the balls flying about on the air current. "Of course, it took awhile for the employees to get used to it, but now they're quite comfortable."

"And you employ everyone in town?" I asked.

"Mostly everyone. But that will change soon."

"What do you mean?"

"I've been planning. Ever since those comics arrived. I've no time for comedy. Laughter never made a mat," she said.

"Who do you mean?" I asked, seeking more information for my new friends. But then Horace rang a loud bell.

"Work time, Andrew," Mrs. Davenport stated. "For you as well. Let me see a new sermon by tomorrow."

"Yes, ma'am," I replied, as I watched the balls randomly bouncing into each other on their way to the top. The sun had not even hit the horizon and the good people of Erasmus were already at work.

Chapter Eight

Jimmy Constantine

I walked out of the Deep and Grubby feeling even more despondent than I had before going in. I now knew the answer to my question: I should go. I could not save Erasmus. I was only one person, and there was nothing I could do or say to help. The turmoil I had been experiencing was exhausting and not getting anyone anywhere.

Knowing the answer was a relief. Sam would arrive as scheduled in his bus at noon, and I would be ready. *Even better,* I thought, *I'll walk across the bridge out of town and flag him down before he even gets here.*

The morning light was climbing in my kitchen window. I ignored the tingling in my spine, and sat and wrote Mrs. Davenport a note:

> *Dear Mrs. Davenport:*
> *I have decided to leave Erasmus. I cannot work in a church that does not appear to believe in God. I would suggest that you remember the second commandment: "Thou*

shalt have no other Gods before me," and the third, "Thou shalt have no golden idols." You seem to be in major violation of these. It wouldn't hurt if you read the other commandments as well.

P.S. The part about the Angel of Death coming to destroy Erasmus is true. I met him in the Quik Clean. He will return on Saturday. I wouldn't make long term plans for anything.

P.S.S. You can have the cream in the refrigerator. It won't travel well.

I placed the note on the counter and looked out the front window. The Erasmus school bus was headed down Main Street. Erasmus had fought long and hard to keep its two-room schoolhouse so their children could receive their whole K–12 education in town. From what I had heard, no one ever left Erasmus. No one except Agnes Davenport had ever crossed the bridge out of town. I too was looking forward to the world on the other side.

With my pack on my back, I turned down Main Street and made a left onto Route 35. "Goodbye, Mrs. Davenport. Goodbye, Erasmus." My short stay here had been interesting. I had learned that sometimes, giving up is the right thing to do.

The tingling in my spine was getting stronger. My body was filling with odd, uncomfortably familiar electricity. I saw the bridge up ahead. Soon I would be free. I tried to attribute the tingling to excitement at my imminent liberation and stepped up my pace.

I was about to cross the bridge when I realized I had nothing to remember Erasmus by, no postcards or tee shirts. I reached into my backpack and got my camera. A picture of Erasmus would say a thousand words, I figured, though most of them wouldn't be positive.

The electricity in my body was increasing. Every pore was infused with energy. I turned and faced the Angel of Death, standing behind me, with the bridge in front of him, as I knew he would be.

"So you've decided?" I asked him.

"Me? It gets decided for me," he replied.

"So I failed."

He shrugged. "We all fail at some point."

"I *am* leaving," I told him.

"You are entitled to make that choice," he replied.

"So will you destroy Erasmus?" I asked.

"I will do what I must."

"But why destroy them for my failure?" I asked.

"If I destroy Erasmus, it will be because they have failed," he said emphatically.

"Has it been decided?" I asked.

"Not yet," he replied. "There is still a chance."

"When will you know?" I asked.

"Very soon."

I was about to ask another question when I heard loud splashing noises and shouting below in the river. Below, one of the Constantine boys was heaving rocks into the water, shouting angrily. He was alone, obviously missing school.

Sam's bus would be coming soon, and if I went down to the riverbank, I would miss it. Then I thought about my own childhood. It would have made a difference, if someone had taken a little time for me. Something was clearly bothering this boy.

The path to the river was steep. "Would you watch my backpack?" I asked Death.

He looked at me blankly.

"Please?" I added.

He nodded. I half hiked, half slid down to the river. The boy was Jimmy. I called his name.

He swung around to face me, surprised and a bit scared.

"Jimmy, I'm Andrew Benoit," I called to him as I stumbled along the rocky bank. "The new pastor. Do you remember me?"

It took him a moment to respond. "Yeah, I remember. I'm allowed to be here, you know."

"What's going on?"

At first I thought he might run away. Then he dropped his face to the ground. He was crying.

"Hey, what's wrong?" I asked gently.

"Nothing!" He couldn't make eye contact. Truth was too difficult to conceal.

"Well, shouldn't you be in school?"

He didn't answer. His hands fidgeted in his pockets. Tears were dropping off his cheek, and he had turned his head away.

I picked up a rock and flicked it expertly into the river, skipping it five times, and looked at Jimmy. His clothes did not fit correctly and his shirt was stained. I remembered the shorts I had taken out of the Lost and Found and the rejection I felt when their source was identified publicly. If clothes can make the man, they can break the boy.

"So, is there something about school you'd prefer to avoid?"

Jimmy sniffled and dug at the dirt. "I hate it," he said. "The kids pick on me. Yesterday, one of them tripped me on the way to lunch. I was carrying my tray, and food splattered all over my clothes."

"Ah." I paused. "I know what you mean. When I was your age the bigger kids would get the smaller ones and put them in a trashcan. I was the last one to grow so I ended up in the trash a lot. Once I got ketchup all over my pants. I took them home and washed them before my mother got home."

"You were picked on, too?" Jimmy asked.

"All the time," I replied."

"I hate riding the bus."

"Yeah. I used to walk two miles so I could catch the bus earlier in the route and get a seat before the bullies got on," I told him.

"What good did that do?" he asked.

"Not much, really, to be honest."

"Why do they do it?"

"I don't exactly know," I said. "I think because they're scared too. I think they know that we see them for what they are. Not tough guys at all. They're afraid of being found out."

He looked away and threw a small rock into the water and watched the water ripple.

"But here's the thing, Jimmy. You can't just run or you end up running forever."

We both sat silently. I was aware that no matter what I could say, his situation would not make sense. The world is full of bullies seeking victims. Fortunately for most of us, we end up on different buses. But fear is everywhere.

"Hey!" Jimmy said excitedly. "Do you want to see me dive?" He pointed to several platforms on a tree overlooking a small pond fed by the river. The water looked clear but not very deep.

"I've jumped from the top platform before," he said. "Next time I'm going one more step up."

"Some other time, Jimmy," I said. "Now you should be getting back to school."

"Please?"

"It wouldn't look too good for the new pastor of Erasmus to be contributing to the delinquency of a minor, on the second day on the job, no less. You want me to walk you there?"

"No, I have my bike," he replied. "Besides, my mom says not to go with strangers." He hoisted his bulky pack onto his back.

"She's right on that," I said. "But I'm going to call the school in a few minutes to make sure you made it OK."

"Yeah," he sighed. "I figured."

I watched as he climbed up the hill, picked up his bike, and put on his helmet. He started walking his bike up the road.

Jimmy Constantine was just like me as a child. I remembered that pain, that loneliness. How could I leave now? I knew how he felt, and that put me in a position to do something to help. Maybe I could even help Erasmus. I had the power of knowledge from Death. Not everyone did. And it wasn't too late.

I looked down the road at the bridge that led out of Erasmus. I'd recently been reminded of a promise I'd made as a boy to a man. Now it was time as a man to make a promise to a boy. I would stay in Erasmus until they no longer needed me.

The Angel of Death had abandoned my pack, an issue I'd take up with him at some later point. For now, I put it on, turned around, and headed back to Erasmus. Outside the school I watched as Jimmy parked his bike in the rack and went inside. I made a note to follow up with the principal.

The tingling in my body was gone. I needed a cup of coffee, and instant would do very well.

Chapter Nine

A Prodigal Daughter Returns

The Instant Coffee Cup was busy as I walked up to the counter. Mrs. Davenport may not have been a big supporter, but it was still the only coffee joint in town. John Luther Zwingli had his back to me and was busy wiping the counter.

"Hey," I called. He turned around.

"So. You decided not to leave?"

"Yeah, I figure I can't give up yet."

"Good to have you back. Want a cup of coffee?"

"Sure," I said. "Give me your finest."

John had hung copies of Norman Rockwell's paintings of the Four Freedoms on the walls. Next to each painting was a photograph of the mystics reenacting the scene. I specifically like *Freedom from Want.* The mystics had amassed quite a feast on a large table, and of course each had a full cup of instant coffee. Mae West was holding a large tofu turkey out over the table. I guess the mystics were vegetarians. John noticed me looking at the pictures. "The mystics got bored," he said. "Next time I'll give them Dali to work from."

"Try Miro or Chagall," I said with a laugh. I have never understood modern art.

Someone tapped my shoulder from behind.

"Harpo," I said, turning to face him. "How are you?"

"You came back." He was smiling.

"I made a promise. I had to come back."

"You're the first prophet to return," he said.

"I'm still not sure I can help," I told him. "How can I convince the people to repent by Saturday?"

"You don't have to do it alone," he said. "Remember, they had faith once."

"In what?" I asked.

"I want to show you something. I think you deserve to see it now."

He gestured for me to follow him through the back of the store, where the mystics were busy playing *Trivial Pursuit.* They all had already gotten pink pies. We went down the back stairway and into a small room. Chairs were set up facing the podium in front, and on it stood an open Bible.

“We meet here every night for church,” he explained.

“You don’t ever go to the First Church of Erasmus?”

“Too cold,” he said, and laughed a bit.

“I see your point.”

He opened a door that led to a dimly lit hallway. I could barely see as we walked but could feel the cold air against the stone walls.

“Simon,” Harpo murmured, as he tapped lightly on a doorway at the end of the hall. “Simon, it’s Harpo. I’ve brought the prophet.”

The door opened slowly and Harpo entered. I stopped in surprise as his footsteps crunched loudly. I looked down. Rice Krispies. The floor was covered with a thick layer of Rice Krispies.

“It’s the alarm system,” said Harpo. “If an intruder got in here Simon would know by the first snap. By crackle they’d be history.”

I crunched into the room behind him. Ahead, a glass coffin containing the figure of a woman sat on a platform in the center of the room. As I got closer I could see that her skin was smooth and unblemished and perfect in tone. She was perfectly groomed and looked peaceful. The smell of roses permeated the air.

"Who is she?"

Harpo was standing back in the shadows and I could barely see him as he answered. "She, my great and noble prophet, is Annie Cotter, the Incorruptible."

Incorruptibles were saints who did not corrupt, or decay, after death, such as St. Bernadette and St. Francis. St. Catherine of Siena too, but her head was removed from her body and taken to another church. The perks of sainthood are not always attractive.

I stepped forward to get a closer look. A figure emerged out of the shadows and reached out a hand to stop me.

"Andrew," said Harpo, as he reappeared from the darkness. "This is Simon, the Knight Templar."

Despite the dim light I could see that Simon was a gaunt figure in a white tunic with a large cross on it. His moustache draped over his chin on either side. His shoulders sank, and he seemed weary. As he stared at me, I could see deep shadows worn into the wrinkled skin under his eyes.

"A Knight Templar?" I asked. "I thought they had been disbanded. They got too powerful."

"They were disbanded." Simon spoke slowly and softly. "My ancestors managed to get away and kept the tradition, each fully aware of and dedicated to achieving what was expected of him."

I wasn't so certain I could do the same, promises to my father notwithstanding. "I am Polaris," I had told him. "I will guide them." But not all people want to be guided. He'd been right about that.

"Why did you come to Erasmus?" I asked.

"For her," he said, pointing to the immaculately preserved woman in the coffin.

"Who is she?" I asked.

"Annie Cotter," he answered. "The first wife of Erasmus Cotter. When she died, the town plunged deep into despair." Harpo nodded silently next to me.

This sounded like Eva Peron. "So what happened?" I asked. Clearly Erasmus had not become the setting for a Broadway musical.

"She worked tirelessly to help the people of Erasmus. She stopped by every house—even the Davenports'. Some say the Davenports would have died out then if not for her. Those who can recall her remember the calm and peace that she brought into a room. One man, now over ninety, recalls being in a hospital bed. She walked in and her warmth and light illuminated the walls. Ironically, because of her no one died in Erasmus during the flu epidemic. Annie was the only casualty—she died a year later from exhaustion. When they went to bury her, she had not decayed. The strong perfume of roses emanated from her body."

I'd noticed the floral bouquet when we walked in. "So, she truly is an Incorruptible," I whispered.

Yes," said Harpo. "This is how the town's faith was renewed. When they realized that Annie would not truly die and leave them, they began to believe again."

"But now. . . ."

"Well, when Mrs. Davenport arrived she set out to destroy Annie. She believes she succeeded. We hid her down here, but even if Mrs. Davenport finds out that Annie is here, she would not be able to get her."

"That's my job," Simon said gravely. Mrs. Davenport represented nothing more to him than a modern-day dragon, and he'd think nothing of slaying her.

"So you see, Andrew, there is hope," said Harpo. He turned to Simon, who appeared to be wearying of our presence. Harpo gestured me to follow him out the door.

"Goodbye, Simon," I called into the shadows.

"Goodbye, prophet."

Outside the door I stood shaking Rice Krispies from my shoe. "Faith is hard to see," I said.

"Always," he responded.

Annie Cotter had brought faith to Erasmus. Mrs. Davenport had tried to take it away. How could I make faith more visible? I would need to find a source of light. I just hoped people would follow.

* * *

Back in my little kitchen, I tore up the note I'd written to Mrs. Davenport, feeling as I did it a renewed sense of purpose. I glanced at the clock. Though it was only eight PM, it seemed much later. I looked at the calendar on the wall. Soon it would be Saturday. I fell asleep the moment my head hit the pillow, but didn't dream. The rabbit must have taken the night off. He'd looked like he needed rest.

The next morning the dogwood tree was in bloom, magnificent in the morning sunlight. Well rested, I reminded myself that there is beauty and faith in Erasmus, you just have to know where to look. I picked up my freshly brewed coffee and walked into the church.

The light was on. A figure sat huddled, praying, in a pew in the corner. "Hello," she said, as I walked past. Her voice was melodious. Her honey-brown hair hung over her shoulders. She was dressed plainly in an embroidered white shirt and jeans. Her beauty had nothing to do with makeup. She smiled. "I just needed some encouragement from God."

"Well," I said, "you've come to the right place." I wasn't so positive, but it seemed like the right thing to say. "By the way, how did you get in?" I clearly remembered locking the door the night before.

"I have a key."

I considered this for a moment. "You're Agnes Davenport, aren't you?" I asked.

"Yes, I am."

"I'm Andrew Benoit, Agnes," I said. "The new pastor. Welcome home."

"So they finally followed through on that. I put in that request almost ten years ago," she said.

"You requested the pastor?"

"Yes. I knew it was wrong for my mother to be giving the sermons."

"Then you brought me here."

"Yes," she replied thoughtfully, "I suppose I did." She stood. She was shorter than I and possessed a gentleness that made me feel I should protect her, a feeling I'd often had for my mother. But I could tell that Agnes had her own light and was not merely reflecting that of others. Sometimes when we seek to protect, we end up covering God's light. Agnes didn't need protection.

"What happened with your store?" I asked.

"Oh," she laughed. "That all seems so long ago."

"Was it?" She didn't look that old. It wasn't like she was Amelia Earhart resurfacing at age one hundred.

"Well, five years. But it just seems longer."

I knew the feeling. My few days in Erasmus already felt like an eternity.

"Was it just a really long line at the lunch counter?" I tried humor again.

"No," she said, "more than that. I've been traveling. It's a long story," she said. "We might want to sit down." We did. She turned sideways to face me. Agnes had the ability to make eye contact without making it feel threatening. Instead she made it seem holy.

"I never wanted the store to begin with," she said. "Mother wanted me to follow in her high heels and go into business. I built the store across the bridge because it was outside Erasmus. That seemed to work for a while, but I wasn't happy."

"Why?"

"Well," she said, dropping her gaze in thought. "I met someone."

"Who?" I asked.

"Jack Paper," she said. "You probably know him as Jackie Paper."

"Yes." Now I knew what had replaced the painted wings and giant's rings. Agnes Davenport had. "I didn't know he was real, though," I mentioned.

"Everything's based on something," she said cryptically. "Did you really think anyone could make up something like that?

"I guess not." I suppose truth usually is stranger than fiction. Peter, Paul, and Mary had always claimed it was just a children's song. Now I knew why. They were protecting Puff.

"Anyway, we met when his car broke down in Erasmus," she continued. "He stayed in town for a while, and every day we would meet for lunch or coffee."

"At the Instant Coffee Cup?" I asked.

"Yes," she replied. "It was the only place I knew my mother would not be."

"And then what?" I questioned.

"Well, Jack promised to show me the world and I decided to see it. One day we went for lunch and just never came back. For a while it was great. We traveled all over the world. We took sculpture classes in Italy. We made a new arm for the Pietà. But there were problems. I found out Jack was using drugs."

"It was never Puff who was using, was it?"

"No," she replied. "It was never Puff."

"I'm sorry," I said. "I didn't know."

"Well, Jack was used to noble kings and princes bowing down whenever Puff and he would arrive. Pirate ships didn't lower their flags for just Jack."

"He was nothing without the dragon," I said.

"No," she replied. "But that's how he felt. And one day I realized that he had just abandoned Puff without an explanation. I figured he would eventually do the same to me. I confronted him."

"And?"

"He agreed that he needed to go seek closure with Puff, and I agreed that I needed to go home and resolve things with my mother."

"Did he work it out with Puff?" I asked.

"I don't think so," she said, and her voice sounded sad. "I think he got distracted. I last got word that he was seen down by the river with someone named Suzanne. She was feeding him tea and oranges that came all the way from China."

"Do you love him?" I asked.

"No," she replied. "I loved the idea of adventure. And now I have come home to talk to my mother. I realized that I could travel all over the world and never really face what I needed to face. Every situation I ran into was symbolic of things I hadn't resolved. Sooner or later you have to come home."

I admired her ability to identify what she must do. And I'll admit I was glad to hear that Jack Paper was out of the picture. I liked what I'd seen of Agnes so far, and figured Jack could be tough competition, especially if the dragon got involved. I don't like reptiles and I don't own any fireproof clothes.

She was looking out the window. I followed her line of sight. She was gazing at the dogwood tree in full bloom in the field.

"Do you see that tree?" she asked.

"Yes," I replied. "It's beautiful."

"My parents planted that tree when I was born. It was a symbol of their love for me," she said.

"Is your father still alive?" I asked.

"Yes," she said. "We keep in touch. He just got tired of my mother wanting more money. He said she stopped loving him. He said she stopped loving anyone." She paused. "I think he was right."

"So you came home," I said.

"Yes," she replied. "I couldn't work it out from a distance."

"I'm impressed," I said. I was truly impressed. The world is full of people who climb every mountain and ford every stream in search of wholeness, but I think Agnes was right. Eventually you have to come home.

"Thank you." She glanced at her watch. "I need to go," she said, standing up. I stood as well.

"Good luck, Agnes. I'll be praying for you."

"Thank you, Andrew. I would appreciate that."

"You're welcome." I opened the door for her and smiled as she turned to leave. She smiled back. It was more than enough to make my day.

I watched as she walked down the church steps and over to the path to Davenport Industries. At the gate she stopped, read the sign requesting money, then vaulted neatly over the top. The yellow lights flashed brightly. Sirens sounded. Dogs began barking. The still of morning was totally shattered by the shrill Davenport Industries' alarm system. Agnes Davenport had come home.

Chapter Ten

When is a Door Not a Door?

"Agnes Davenport is back," I said, sipping my foam cup of instant.

"You saw her?" asked John Luther Zwingli.

"Yes, and spoke with her," I said. "She's quite a woman." I smiled.

"You like her, huh?"

"I didn't say that," I replied sheepishly. "You just don't meet many like her."

"I don't know her well. She used to come in here with a guy. He was kind of strange. Gave me all this junk," John said as he reached in a drawer and pulled out some string and sealing wax and other fancy stuff. I guess Jackie was trying to make friends in the only way he knew.

"She's come home to reconcile with her mother," I told him.

"I hope she's got lots of money," he said, then paused. "No, that's not fair. I don't want to be nasty about it."

"Well, it seems like she'll have a tough time." I'd learned the hard way that the enemy can come from within. As a child I'd always thought the Benoit family formed one perfect unit. United we stood, never to be permanently divided, until my father left for the last time.

"Mrs. Davenport is pretty cold," John said, shivering. "Some people don't really want light, Andrew."

"Well, if anyone can do it, I think Agnes has a pretty deep connection to God," I said.

"I hope so," he replied.

"Hey, have you seen Harpo?" I asked.

"He's downstairs," John replied. "They're having a service. They have one every morning."

"Thanks." I walked to the back of the coffee shop. It was deserted. The mystics were absent from their usual table. I tiptoed down the stairs to the basement. The mystics sat facing the front with heads bowed silently and candles burning on both aisles. I could smell the faint scent of roses. I took a seat at the back of the room.

Curly stood in the silence and spoke. "We are at a crossroads of faith. The road here was easy. It was a path we idealistically followed. I remember that when I first signed up I figured it was going to be an adventure. I forgot that adventures mean challenges."

The group murmured affirmations and nodded their heads.

"We have hit a wall, my friends," he continued. "We have much to do and less than a week to do it. The wall is high and thick and I do not see a way. We build walls to protect us, but then they keep everyone else out. Faith must provide a door, and I am losing faith," he said, and he sat down, placing his head in his hands.

Lucy stood. "Faith *is* the door in the wall." She sat down and placed her hand on Curly's shoulder. He turned to her, and she smiled and nodded her head.

The mystics remained silent for a while. They were seeking answers and facing uncertainty. Then Harpo stood and walked to the front. He placed his hands on the podium and looked out over his congregation.

"Yes, we are at a difficult place. The darkness of fear has crept into Erasmus and blanketed faith. We have but a moment to change the course of the future. We are people and we are only human and yet we are seeking to do the work of God.

"When I was younger, I left home to search for God. I followed what I thought was God's light but never seemed to find God. I got frustrated. I was angry. But I eventually realized that if I returned and stayed in this place, that light of God would find me here.

"We have always found faith in the sunrise. In the sounds of the birds. In the breeze. And in each other. Now we must find it in ourselves. Let us be the door." He sat down. The group remained in silence for a few minutes. A small ray of sunlight filtered through the basement window and reflected the swirling candle smoke.

Finally Harpo rose, shook Mae West's hand, and continued walking around the room, shaking hands. There were a few people I recognized from the streets of Erasmus. Some looked at me and quickly turned away. Others stared, expecting some reaction. After all, I was the pastor from the church of Davenport.

"Welcome, Andrew," Harpo said. I saw the faces relax. By this time all had turned their heads to see me.

"Thank you, Harpo," I said. "I liked what you said."

"Thanks," he said. "I hope it works."

"We have a lot of work to do," I said.

"Yes we do," he replied. "Time to get going."

After the congregation dispersed, we sat down at the mystics' table. Mae West produced a large chalkboard and some chalk. John Wayne served cups of freshly re-hydrated coffee. I stood at the front with the chalk in my hand. I hoped this wouldn't be anything like football, with all those X's and O's that never meant anything to me.

Taking on Death was going to require strategy. We needed to persuade a whole town that their future depended not only on dressing in sackcloth themselves, but also providing similar attire for their children and livestock. We were short on time, so I figured the stitching didn't have to be perfect.

If we each took on a certain portion of the population, we could spread the word. I broke the town into areas and asked for volunteers under each. I felt a little like Paul Revere without the horse or the famous call but with a few mystics. Frankly, I didn't want a horse; the last thing we needed was another farm animal on which to put sackcloth.

"Andrew, do you really think that this will work?" Harpo asked.

"We will be the door through the wall," I replied. He smiled.

"We're going to have to work hard," I shouted. "Can we do it?"

"Yes!"

I wanted to tell them we should win one for the Gipper, but the Gipper was dead and we were doing this for the living. Then it occurred to me. "Win it for Jimmy Constantine," I called out.

The mystics walked up the steps. As they passed me each offered some encouragement.

"Good job, Andrew."

"Nice work, Coach."

"Loved it."

John Wayne was the last to leave. He was dressed in a tie-dyed tee shirt that had a love symbol on the front. He wore a peace necklace and a Daniel Boone coonskin hat. I couldn't tell him he was mixing centuries.

"Andrew, I don't know how to tell you this," he said, "but you know that speech that Harpo gave?"

"Yeah," I said. "It was great."

"He has used it in every town we have been to."

"And?" I questioned. John stopped halfway up the stairs and turned his head.

"It never works," he replied.

* * *

I walked out of the Instant Coffee Cup. Less than a week ago the town of Erasmus had meant nothing to me. Now that had changed. It was no longer just a pit stop between the start and the finish.

Main Street reminded me of the old Westerns. Where was Sheriff Will Cain from *High*

Noon or Matt Dillon from *Gunsmoke*? Would Miss Kitty and countless other admirers watch from the safety of balconies or behind windows? I had to save the town. Death was coming in on the noon train. We would stand facing each other. But can you kill Death? Perhaps laughter would work.

"Take my wife . . . please!" No, too dangerous, what with "wife" and "life" sounding so similar. Humor wasn't going to work. I guess I'd have to rely on faith.

"Andrew," called a female voice. Miss Kitty?

"Andrew!" she repeated, waking me out of my daydream. It was Mrs. Carstairs.

"Yes, hello, Mrs. Carstairs."

"I have good news."

"What is it?"

"Well," she said, "I've been learning a new song to play. I'm very excited."

"That's great," I told her. "Maybe you can play it next Sunday." *Provided,* I thought, *there is a next Sunday.*

"Well, maybe."

"What is the new piece of music?"

“Chopsticks,” she replied, bustling off down Main Street.

Well, if nothing else, church would be interesting.

I looked at my watch. It was already 2:30 PM. The day had flown by. Down Main Street I saw Jimmy Constantine walk into Bill and Betty’s Toy Store. This would be a good opportunity to follow up with him and see how things were going.

The bell rang on the door as I opened it. Bill and Betty’s Toy Store looked and felt like a store you might have seen in a television show about the fifties. There were wind-up gliders, cap guns, and Zombie dolls. Jimmy was examining the bike accessories.

“Hey, Jimmy,” I said.

“Hi, Pastor Benoit.”

“How are things?”

Jimmy looked at me, and I could tell he wanted to say something specific. He paused for a moment. I sensed that he had changed his mind.

“I’m fine. I’m going to ride my bike in the Erasmus Day parade.”

"What's Erasmus Day?" I asked. I'd wondered about that ever since seeing it in one of the handouts from the town museum.

"It's to celebrate the founding of Erasmus. This Friday. We get the day off from school."

So on Friday, the whole town would be celebrating. This could be the opportunity I needed.

"How's everything going at school?" I asked.

"All right," Jimmy shrugged.

"Are the other kids still picking on you?" I asked. He was quiet.

"You know what? The bullies only help make you stronger," I said.

"I don't want to be stronger," he said. "I just want a few friends."

"You will make friends. And eventually you'll begin to listen to yourself and ignore what people like that say."

"Hey," he said, smiling. "What do you think of these?" He pointed to some flashy ornaments for his bike. "For the parade, I mean."

"Cool," I said. "They look great."

"Yeah, I like them." He fumbled in his pocket for change. He pulled out a pile that consisted of gum wrappers, two pens, a few dollars, and some change.

Please God, I thought, *let this boy have some money.* He looked at the price tag, picked through his money, then slowly put the ornaments back on the wall. His shoulders slumped.

"So," I said. "Those are the best?"

"Yeah," he said. "Are you going to be in the parade?"

"Yes, someday," I said, taking the streamers off the wall. "And I've been meaning to decorate my bike, but I'll be too busy to be in the parade this year. Would you like to borrow these streamers on Friday? You're welcome to."

"Really?" he asked.

"Sure," I said. "C'mon."

Together we walked up to the cash register. Betty stood behind an old manual register. She poked the buttons, took the money, and handed me a handwritten receipt. I handed Jimmy the streamers.

"Good luck," I said.

"Thanks, Pastor Benoit!" he said. He was smiling. I knew it wasn't just the gift.

"Call me Andrew," I said.

"Thanks, Andrew," he said.

"You're welcome, Jimmy," I said. We walked out the door and stopped by his bike. He placed the package in his backpack, swung his leg over the seat, and rode off down the street. I could swear I saw Miss Kitty wave to me from the balcony of one of the buildings. Women love a guy who is good with children.

It was Wednesday afternoon. We had some time to get ready. On Friday I'd have a chance to speak to the whole town. I was a bit worried about John Wayne's words and I was confused by what Simon had said, but if I could take to the whole town the feeling I'd just experienced by helping Jimmy, I felt grace could prevail.

As I approached my house I saw a figure seated on a branch of the dogwood tree. It looked like Agnes Davenport. I wondered how the reconciliation process was going. Agnes was helping the cause. If Mrs. Davenport could repent, then there was hope, and hope was a door in a wall.

I spent most of Wednesday afternoon planning. A good plan would get us through that wall. Faith is fine, but a plan is better, and I needed to make the most out of what little we had. Erasmus was perched on the precipice, and right now it felt like only a small strand of faith was holding it back. The strand consisted of a Knight Templar, a young boy, a few mystics, a coffee shop owner, and the daughter of the most evil woman in town.

I looked out at the dogwood tree. Agnes was no longer sitting in the branches. Maybe Jack Paper had returned with more fancy stuff. I wasn't really sure what her plan with her mother had been, but I hoped it worked.

The phone rang. I hadn't had any phone calls while I was in Erasmus. The size of the town made face-to-face contact more efficient, and I didn't really know anyone outside of Erasmus who would be calling.

"Andrew?" I recognized the voice. It was Agnes.

"How did it go with your mother?" I asked.

"Not well," she said. "That's why I'm calling. I wanted to fill you in."

"Do you want to talk in person?" I asked.

"Sure," she said. "That would be even better. How about at the Instant Coffee Cup?"

"Half an hour?" I asked.

"Sure," she replied. "That would be good."

"See you there."

I hung up the phone. I was smooth. I was cool. I was also nervous about meeting Agnes, a sure sign that I liked her.

* * *

"Hey, John."

"Hey, Prophet," he replied. "You're beginning to become quite a regular around here."

"Guess so."

"What's up?" he asked.

"I'm meeting Agnes."

"So how's that going?"

"What going?" I said, irritated.

"Ah, you're really just doing it for the coffee, is that it?"

"Actually, I'm getting used to the stuff. Funny how that is."

"No accounting for taste," he said, and went back to wiping the counter.

"Hey John, you ever been married?" I asked.

"Once," he replied.

"How was it?" I asked.

"Great at times. Tough at others."

"Did you have kids?" I asked.

"No."

"You got divorced?"

"Yeah," he said. "It was the saddest day of my life. But I knew it was the right move."

"Do you still keep in touch?"

"I hear from her now and then." He paused. "Boy, you have a lot of deep questions for a guy just looking for a cup of joe."

The bell on the door rang and Agnes Davenport walked in.

"Hey, Andrew," she said. "Hi, John Luther, how are you?"

"Just fine. Welcome back, lovely lady."

"Thanks. I just got back a few days ago. I missed your coffee."

"Tell that to the prophet," he said.

"Prophet?" she asked. John pointed to me.

“Yeah, that’s what they call me,” I told her.

“Why?” she asked.

“It’s a long story,” I replied. “Hey, do you want to go for a walk?”

“Sure,” she said.

I turned to John. “Two cups of joe . . . to go.”

As we walked the streets of Erasmus, I explained what had brought me here, what had happened so far, and what I thought we were facing. It was the first time in a long time I felt I could be open. Agnes was a great listener, just asking questions for clarification. She accepted my whole story without hesitation. Then I realized I had been so immersed in my own story that I had forgotten to ask her what had happened with Mrs. Davenport.

“Well, of course mother was surprised to see me,” she said, “and setting off every alarm in her building didn’t help. But I always wanted to do that.”

“And?”

Agnes sighed. “She was really stubborn. She said she was glad she had me back and wondered when I would start working again at the convenient. After all, we were losing money."

"So you didn't make any progress at all?"

"No, Andrew," she said sadly. "I'm afraid not. I don't know if it's even possible. She's so sure of herself, so sure of what she wants. This," Agnes said as she pointed to a trail leading into the woods, "is my favorite way to walk to the store. It's a shortcut."

"Really?"

"Yes," she replied, "but it passes a beautiful pond."

"I'll have to walk up it someday," I said, "whenever I leave Erasmus."

Chapter Eleven

Ninety-five Pieces on the Wittenberg Door

I went to bed early. I needed to be well rested for the task ahead. I woke early Thursday morning. It looked like it was going to be a beautiful day. The sun was just creeping up on the horizon, and I could feel the gentleness of its touch as light radiated in my bedroom.

I drank coffee from my lucky mug and looked over my plans for the day. We would have to accomplish a great deal in the next twenty-four hours. My first task was to find the mystics and get organized. We were headed into the big game, and we were going up against a foe that had been unbeatable. We were the Bad News Bears taking on the 1927 Athletics or the 1929 Yankees. Take your pick.

I walked down to the Instant Coffee Cup. John Luther Zwingli was standing in front with his hands on his hips. The door had been plastered with signs that read, "Instant Coffee Is Bad for You!" "The Surgeon General Rules Instant Coffee Illegal" and "Instant Oatmeal Is No Better." While I had to admit that there was a certain validity to the messages, I also recognized the significance of their posting. Yellow tape was stretched across the doorway, and a "Closed Due to Health Violations" notice was prominently displayed. Horace Bogardus, Health Department Commissioner, had signed it.

"What happened here?" I asked.

"She's closed us down, shut the water off. A man can't run an instant coffee bar without water." He sighed in resignation.

"John, you can't give up."

"No, kid, I can't give up, but I might give in."

"Give me a chance, John."

"It's not about you." He started to pull the sticky yellow tape from the doorway.

"Have you seen the mystics?"

"Downstairs, packing up. Or maybe gone already."

"Thanks." I hurried to the back stairway and down into the small worship room.

“Harpo? Mae?” I called out. “Is anyone here?” Silence. The mystics were gone. I needed to find them.

The smell of roses reminded me not to lose hope. Annie Cotter. Erasmus had its own saint; surely that was reason enough to maintain faith. What more did we need to have affirmed? She had been preserved beyond physical death, perhaps to show us there is eternal life. I walked down the back hallway to Annie’s room. I knocked softly at first, and when I did not get a response, harder.

“Simon,” I called softly.

There was no answer.

“Simon! It’s me. The prophet.”

The door opened slowly, and I walked into the room, looking down suddenly in surprise. I’d forgotten about the snap, crackle, and pop. One ray of golden sunlight beamed through a crack in the covered window, illuminating the body of Annie Cotter. There was a glow to her skin and a softness in her eyes that belied her more than one hundred years’ entombment.

“Simon?” I called again.

"Yes, prophet." He was standing just beyond the shard of light. He appeared even more exhausted than when I had seen him last. Dust floated in the light that speared the air beside him.

"Simon, you have stayed here all of these years guarding Annie. You have forsaken any other kind of life in exchange for duty. How do you maintain your faith?" I asked.

He looked at me in silence for a long moment. I wanted to tell him that Erasmus was in great trouble. I wanted to say that I could not find the mystics and was afraid I could not do anything to save the town. I wanted to say I was frightened, but duty is an odd call, and I had my own to answer to. I didn't want to worry him.

"I think of God," he said.

"What do you mean?"

"Prophet, you are young," he said. "Someday you will see all that God has given you. But you must let God in yourself first."

"I don't understand," I said.

"You see this?" he asked as he pointed to the focused shaft of light.

"Yes."

"This is God."

"You mean light is God?"

"It is one way to describe God," he replied. "Remember: In the beginning there was Light."

"Yes," I replied. "But then, what is the room?"

"The room is your heart, prophet."

"But it is so dark."

"Only because you allow it to be," he replied.

"But Annie brings light," I said.

"No," he replied. "Annie only provides a way to light."

"But you have guarded her all of your life," I said. "Why?"

"People need something they can see," he answered. "But you must believe in that which you can't see. Then you will be full of light."

Simon spoke simply. I wasn't so sure I felt any more confident then when I came in, but I could tell there was nothing more to talk about. I walked toward the door but turned around at the last minute. I needed to tell someone what I was feeling. "What if I am afraid?"

"This, prophet, is what fear does," he said as he placed his hand in front of the beam of light, followed it all the way up to the hole in the window, and disappeared into the total darkness.

I walked upstairs. The situation did not look good for me or for Erasmus. Mrs. Davenport had closed down the Instant Coffee Cup, the mystics had departed for parts unknown, and John, who was sitting mumbling to himself amidst packing boxes, clearly felt defeated. Agnes had told me she hadn't convinced her mother to change, and she'd been right. The fellowship was crumbling.

"John," I said. "Where have the mystics gone? Did they say anything?"

"Yeah, they said something about the dump yard. They know they cannot stay here anymore." He sipped his cup of instant coffee. It's sad to see the people of Erasmus turn their backs on me, and this place. And to anyone associated with me."

"They're just scared," I said. But I wondered if anyone had seen me entering the Instant Coffee Cup.

"I'm not worried, Andrew. Just disappointed. Anyway, if you what you say is true,

Erasmus won't need a coffee shop much longer. Maybe Erasmus doesn't want to be saved."

I walked out onto the porch. The temperature had been fluctuating wildly lately, and now thunderstorms were predicted. Despite the morning sunshine, a bad weather advisory had been in effect for the end of the week, and it looked like that prediction would come true. How fitting.

"God," I shouted. "You called me. Now I need your help." No answer. *The Angel of Death,* I thought. *Perhaps he would help me.* After all, he was the one who had served my commission. But where could I find him?

Erasmus had two laundromats. The Quik Clean was across the bridge, and the other was in the basement of the Country Cupboard. Try there first.

I scurried down Main Street to the Country Cupboard, walked up to the front door, and was greeted there by Mrs. Carstairs, who opened the door but stood blocking it.

"We're closed," she said. "Sorry." She gently pushed me back across the threshold, locked the door, and pulled down the shade.

"But Mrs. Carstairs," I shouted. She placed the CLOSED sign on the window, and I could hear her loudly humming *Amazing Grace*. I had to get into the laundromat one way or another. I jogged around back. I could hear the rising sounds of Mrs. Carstairs' voice as I climbed through a back window and dropped to the floor. The laundromat had two washing machines and two dryers. A sign-up sheet for the machines had only one name on it: Constantine. A large box of soap sat to one side, and a sign overhead read, "Please empty the lint filter when you are done."

I looked at the washing machines. Both appeared to be in working order. *Look, Death,* I thought, *I need a miracle. How can I reach you?*

"You got me into this!" I shouted into one machine. "You can't just leave me here!" I stuck my head into a machine and shouted, "Death, I need your help!"

The sound reverberated emptily in the cylinder. I looked around for a pencil and piece of paper. Perhaps I could leave Death a note. Finding what I needed, I wrote:

Dear Angel of Death

I need your help. I am lost. Mrs. Davenport has closed the Instant Coffee Cup and I believe I have failed and Erasmus will be destroyed. Can you talk to God? A plague might be helpful.

Something they can see.

Thanks,

Andrew the Prophet

(Andrew Benoit. We met in the Quik Clean.)

I dropped the note down into the empty machine, fished in my pocket for coins, and placed them in the slot. Soap did not seem necessary. The machine started with a loud banging sound, and I could hear scuttling feet up above.

"Who's down there?" Mrs. Carstairs shouted. I felt it best not to answer.

I patted the washing machine on the top. "C'mon, baby, do your stuff." Dixie Manufacturing's finest had never faced such an important task, and I was hoping it was up to it.

"I'm coming down," Mrs. Carstairs shouted. I stepped up onto the dryer and pulled myself back out the window. My exit was impeded by a collision with John Wayne. As with any smaller object colliding with a larger one, I ended up on my seat on the ground.

"What's the hurry, pardner?" he asked.

"John, it's all falling apart. Mrs. Davenport has closed the Instant Coffee Cup. I'm scared I've failed."

"Ah," he said as he reached down to help me up. "You need courage. Courage is being scared to death and saddling up anyway."

"Saddling up?"

"Get back on the trail, Andrew. You've just gotten off for a moment."

"I feel lost."

"Well, remember when you were a child and got off the trail, what were you told to do?"

"Stay where you are."

"Right. If you run around like crazy you'll just get more lost."

"But, John, I've already been lost for a long time."

“In that case you need to look to the past, sort out where you took a wrong turn. Maybe your ancestors can help.”

“My ancestors? I’m not worried about the past, I’m worried about tomorrow,” I said.

“Tomorrow,” John said, stopping to bend one knee and place a foot upon a rock, “is the most important thing in life. Comes unto us at midnight very clean. It’s perfect when it arrives, and it puts itself in our hands. But it requires that we’ve learned something from yesterday.”

“I don’t have much time.”

“Follow me.”

I followed him down the sidewalk and out onto a trail that led through a small woods and into a large junkyard. I had to take two footsteps for every one of John’s. We didn’t speak as we walked. Mostly, despite his philosophizing, he was a quiet man.

Large piles of debris surrounded a small campsite. Discarded Deep and Grubby floor mats were piled in huge mounds on either side. Harpo, Lucy, Mae, Lou, and Curly were seated in a circle, talking quietly.

“Hi there, Andrew,” Harpo said as he got up to greet me. “You look worried.”

“I need help, I feel lost. John said I should look to the past, and brought me here.”

“Join us,” Lucy said, and I walked over and sat down in the circle. “It is time to speak to your ancestors.”

The mystics gathered wood and pine needles in the center of the circle and lit a fire, which crackled and sizzled and smelled of piney resin. The sparks spiraled upward, and the smoke started to form the outlines of human beings.

The first was a man with a raven, perched on his shoulder, with a bun in its mouth. The man was covered with nettles.

“Saint Benedict?” I asked.

The next form was that of a woman holding a songbook and inspecting a plant. She was toning, unaware that her presence had entered our sphere.

“Fa-so-la-ti-doh” “Fa-Oh-Oh-Uh-Oh”—she stopped as she noticed the crowd watching.

“Hildegard of Bingen.”

“Saint Francis of Assisi!” I said as I saw the next figure emerge from the smoke. St. Benedict’s raven immediately flew over to St. Francis's shoulder.

The last figure was carrying a shepherd's crook.

"Saint Patrick," I stated.

"These are your ancestors," said Harpo.

"I remember all of you. I used to ask you for help when I was a child. My mother had taught me about you. She believed that each of you could help me."

"Yes, Andrew," Hildegard said.

"And when I couldn't sleep. . . ."

"We chased away the monsters from under your bed," said St. Francis.

"There were monsters under my bed?"

"No, no, but you thought there were."

"We were by your side," St. Patrick said.

"I didn't see you."

"If you had you would have been scared. But we were there."

"Really?" I asked.

"Yes."

"I felt lost then," I said. "And I feel lost now."

"We've all been there. At one time we were only human, Andrew," St. Patrick said. We didn't know when we started that we would end up as saints. We just did what we believed in. It was our call."

"I had fine clothes once. I was a noble," St. Francis stated.

"I loved a woman. I gave up great wealth. I was almost killed," said St. Benedict.

"And I was a sickly child. I didn't know what to do or where to go with my visions," Hildegard reminded me. "But I loved music and plants. I was never really recognized in my own time, Andrew. Our power," she said, "was and is truth."

"I must be real," I said. "I must speak the truth."

"Yes," they replied. "Truth cannot be defeated—only silenced. And even then it finds a voice. You must find the truth, Andrew. What do you want to say?"

"Well, I want to say that Mrs. Davenport is wrong. She thinks she can create faith by closing down anyone who disagrees with her. But she will only create fear."

"Then say that, Andrew," St. Francis said. "To her."

"That will take courage."

"Yes, Andrew. Truth requires courage."

The vapors that formed the outlines of the saints were now fading, and the figures were disappearing.

"Remember, Andrew, at one time we were only human." Their voices trailed off into the darkening morning. I looked around. The mystics were silent. I had to find the truth within and speak it. I had to find my own voice if I expected Erasmus to find its way.

"Guys," I said.

"And gals," added Lucy and Mae.

"And gals," I corrected myself, "I've got something to say."

"You seem excited."

"I am," I said. "I can do this. I can speak the truth." I searched around in the junk piles until I found a partially used pack of sticky notes and an old pen. I held them up.

"I will write a truth on each one."

"Such as?" asked John.

"Mrs. Davenport shouldn't close the Instant Coffee Cup."

"And?"

"Fear isn't the way to succeed."

"That's a good one," they agreed.

"Poor people are equal to wealthy people."

"True," they all said.

I kept writing as they watched, quietly. I wrote one after another, until I had finished the whole packet. Then I stopped and counted. Ninety-five.

"Wow," I said, looking at the stack.

"What?"

"Ninety-five. I have ninety-five pieces. Ninety-five truths."

"May we see them?"

"Sure," I replied. "But you'll have to come with me to the Deep and Grubby."

"What?"

"Follow me."

We formed a little parade. When we got to the Deep and Grubby, I stuck the sticky notes all over the door.

"The Wittenberg Door!" the mystics sang out.

"Yes," I said. "The Wittenberg Door."

We returned to the junkyard, the mystics with stunned looks on their faces. Our circle had barely formed again when we were interrupted by the sound of a man's voice calling over the piles of old discarded floor mats.

"*Deep and Grubby Gram* for Mr. Andrew Benoit!" The balding head of Horace Bogardus appeared, bobbing among the rubble. "Deep and Grubby Gram for Mr. Andrew Benoit," he repeated as he approached. "You Andrew Benoit?"

"Horace, you know I am."

"Right," he replied. "Well, then, I can save you the trouble of reading this. Mrs. Davenport wants to meet you today. At noon."

"She read the notes?"

"She's angry, Andrew," he said darkly, "and she won't be alone."

"Neither will Andrew," shouted the circle. "We'll be with him."

"Sorry to put you in this situation, Andrew. It's just my job." He scurried away through the piles.

"Andrew, we will make the town change. Never underestimate the ability of a group of small people to change the world," Harpo said.

"That's Margaret Mead," I said. "But it's a small group of people."

"I always thought she said it because she worked with Pygmies," he said, scratching his head.

"We'll help you," Curly said. "We can find weapons here, in the junkyard!"

"Here's an old whoopee cushion," Lou Costello called out.

"And a couple of pillows for pillow fights," said Mae.

"That always ends with someone getting hurt," I reminded her.

"Oh," she said. "Right."

"I'll challenge her to a wine making contest," Lucy said, rolling over a discarded barrel.

"Well, whatever makes sense," I said. I looked at that group of familiar faces now supporting me in my darkest hour.

"You know," I told them, "I've always relied on you."

"What do you mean?" they asked.

"We moved around so much when I was a kid that I had a hard time making friends. I wasn't like Jamie. I'd come home and watch television and you were always there."

"We were your friends?"

"Yes, well, your namesakes were." I paused. "You made me laugh. And sometimes, when I couldn't sleep, I'd watch old movies. I'd laugh until I fell asleep. That way I didn't feel alone."

"I'm glad we could help," said Harpo.

"And now," said Lucy. "We must help now. But we have work to do."

The noise level increased as they discussed their plans. I'd just started to join in when I felt a hand on my shoulder. It was Agnes.

"Andrew, I heard," she said. "I tried to talk with her. For a moment I thought I was getting through. But she kept saying that she had to take care of the town, that they would be lost without her."

"She's afraid." I stated.

"When she saw the Post-It notes on the door she got very angry. I've never seen her like that. She blames you, she thinks you did it."

"I am sorry you're upset, Agnes," I said. Her eyes were filled with tears. "But I did do it. I met the saints last night."

"The saints?"

"Yes," I said. "Saint Benedict, Saint Hildegard, Saint Francis of Assisi, and Saint Patrick. They challenged me to speak the truth."

"Ah, now I see," she nodded slowly. "The notes on the Wittenberg Door."

"Yes, that's why I put them there. I have been silent a long time." I paused, and then said, "My mother believed in the saints. That they would protect me."

"I have always prayed to Saint Thérèse of Lisieux. She is supposed to bring a rose when she answers your prayer," said Agnes.

"Has she ever answered?"

"Not yet," she replied. "Andrew, I will stand with you."

"I wish I could give you all the roses in the world," I said. I eyed a group of flowers growing next to a rusty car. I picked one and gave it to Agnes. It was a daisy. "This is from me, Agnes," I said. "I've never been a rose. I'm just ordinary."

"A daisy is never ordinary, Andrew. Never."

"Thanks, Agnes," I said. "That means a lot."

All around us, the mystics were rooting through piles of rubble. Curly had found an Instant Pudding cream pie still in its box. *Probably had an expired date,* I thought. Lucy and John Wayne were connecting mismatched wheels to a vat. Harpo had found a derelict harp and was picking out a melody. Mae West was using a plastic bucket to fill a *Super Soaker* water pistol.

The hands on the clock ticked toward noon. I eyed the team that was going to accompany me. I sure hoped Margaret Mead was right.

"We must go," I said. "It's almost noon."

Storm clouds gathered in the sky above as we hit Main Street. "Storm's brewing," murmured John, the only sound as we walked silently toward

Deep and Grubby. Window shades opened and closed quickly as we passed. The energy we shared felt new to me. We were a team.

As we approached Deep and Grubby, I could see Mrs. Davenport standing on the front steps. She was surrounded by all of the Deep and Grubby employees, and not one of them was smiling. I saw a large handful of yellow sticky notes in Mrs. Davenport's ring hand, but the gleam was dulled by the sticky notes and shadows created by the impending storm.

We faced her. "I am here, Mrs. Davenport," I yelled.

"Yes," she replied. "With a group of riffraff."

"With friends."

"Mother," Agnes called out. "Stop this. It has gotten out of hand."

"I have the whole town to look after."

"These people here are part of the town. You can't just get rid of everyone who disagrees with you."

I looked around me. Harpo was starting to strum his harp. Lou had the cream pie and was ready to launch it. Lucy was standing in the vat and challenging Mrs. Davenport to join her.

"I will not leave Erasmus," I shouted.

"I will not let you stay," Mrs. Davenport shouted back. The throng of Deep and Grubby employees, who wore suits of Deep and Grubby Mats as armor, started walking slowly down the steps toward us. Lou's trigger finger was slipping on the cream pie. Harpo had increased the tempo. Mae had her water pistol aimed. I looked at the mass of people in front of me and recalled that they had recently been sitting quietly, listening to my sermon.

"God, please, help us," I said.

At that moment, the sky opened up. With a loud crack, the dark clouds sent a lightning bolt scissoring though the sky directly into the roof of the Deep and Grubby. Flames erupted from the building, and the assembled crowd stared for a moment in shock at the conflagration.

"John, help me fill this vat so we can dump it on the fire!" Lucy shouted. They ran to a nearby hose. Lou launched his cream pie into the inferno. Mae West hit it with all the force of a Super Soaker.

Bucket brigades were formed, and lines drawn between enemies were erased in the face of emergency. Deep and Grubby employees formed supportive liaisons with mystics. Horace Bogardus drove in on the fire engine.

"Mom," Agnes said as she carried a bucket, "I'm sorry."

Mrs. Davenport turned away from her.

"Mom," Agnes said. "Look at them. All these people. You no longer have to take care of them. They are taking care of you."

Mrs. Davenport turned, and I could see there were tears in her eyes. Agnes reached her arms out and embraced her mother as the flames subsided. They walked out to the dogwood and sat together while the townspeople of Erasmus, now united, cheered the teamwork that had saved at least part of the building.

"He came though for me," I said to John Luther Zwingli.

"They all came through," he replied.

"No, God, I mean," I said. "God destroyed the Deep and Grubby."

John looked at me with a perplexed stare. "No, Andrew, it was a lightning bolt." He walked over to help Mrs. Carstairs, who was starting an aggressive clean-up detail.

Sure it was, I said to myself. Whatever. Because I could save Erasmus.

"You know," I said to Agnes, "somehow your mother didn't seem as cold as usual. Maybe it was the fire."

She shot me a quick glare.

"Sorry," I said.

"It wasn't that," she said.

"Why, what happened?"

"Before I came to the junkyard I decided to try again to make her see the light. But talking still wouldn't work, so I decided to use a little reverse psychology. I figured that if she wanted me to go into business, I'd go into business. I told her I could make a few dollars by cutting down that dogwood tree and selling it for firewood. She was shocked. I picked up an axe and started walking out the door when she stopped me."

"What did she say?"

"She accused me of not caring about anything. She reminded me what that tree represented."

"And?"

"I told her it was taking up valuable space; a commercial building could be constructed there. Rent or profit could be collected. She could hardly argue with that."

"So what happened?"

"She followed me out to the dogwood, gazing at the blossoms. I knew how much the tree meant to her. I picked up the axe and swung it. . . ." She became silent.

I stood quietly next to Agnes. I didn't have anything to say. I waited for her to continue.

"Mother grabbed the handle. 'That tree is sacred!' she cried. 'It was planted for you, it is part of you and part of me; it represents the love we have for you.'" Agnes smiled. "Poor mother. It took getting to the point of destruction for her to see it."

Chapter Twelve

Death Gets Serious

John Luther Zwingli ran up to us. "I'm glad I found the two of you," he said, out of breath.

"What's up?" I asked.

"It's Jimmy Constantine. He was racing his bike behind his house with his brothers. They had set up a few ramps to jump . . ."

"What happened?" asked Agnes, eyes wide with fear.

". . . and he took a bad fall. Somehow he got twisted around in the air and landed on his back."

"Is he going to be all right?" I asked.

"We don't know yet, Andrew," John replied. "But it doesn't look good."

"Let's go," I said.

We ran down the street toward the little hospital. I could feel my heart pounding and the adrenaline rushing inside. But I was aware of more. I could sense strong electricity surging in my body. I knew what it was. Death was back.

A crowd had gathered in the emergency waiting room. Mrs. Davenport stood next to the

Constantine boys, holding them tightly to her side. Agnes walked over and hugged Peter, the smallest.

Through a window in the swinging door I could see a small group of doctors huddled around a gurney. When they moved, I could see Jimmy's face contorted in pain. He didn't seem to be speaking or moving in response to the doctor's questions. Mrs. Constantine was standing by his side, crying. I looked around. The other Constantine boys looked terrified.

The tingling in my body grew stronger. The now-familiar energy filled my body. The Angel of Death was nearby. He was toying with me and with Erasmus. He would take the people one by one. He had been playing with me all along. I remembered him standing by the bridge near Jimmy Constantine earlier in the week. If I hadn't showed up, he would have taken him. Jimmy would have dived from above the platform and been killed. It was that simple. Death wasn't going to abide by the rules.

I ran outside and down Main Street. Death wasn't going to win this one. I had more to say now; I would not be silent. I ran up the steps to the church and threw the door open.

"You are in here somewhere," I shouted. "I can feel you." The tingling resonated throughout my whole body. My feet and hands were burning.

"Where are you?" I yelled. The charge in my body was growing stronger. It was equaled by my growing anger. "Where are you?" I shouted again, even louder this time. "I know you're in here!" My voice reverberated off the stone walls of the church. I could have filled the space with anger.

Then I saw him, in the chapel, praying. He was kneeling on the floor and looking up into the light. Slowly he rose and sat on the front pew with his head bowed in his hands. He was crying softly.

I ran to face him. "You don't care, do you?" I yelled. "You pretend to cry but you don't care what happens to us," I shouted. "You're toying with us."

"No, you're wrong," he said, his words mixed with tears. I almost felt sorry for him. But a boy was dying, and whom could I blame?

Death looked up at me, and then he began to grow. The black cloth, the shroud, and all his vestments billowed as they increased in size. He stood before me, his figure now almost filling the chapel. The folds of his cloak became alive, flowing with an energy that was massive in its force. I was nearly knocked unconscious by what I saw.

Within the creases, I saw people fighting, children screaming, flames engulfing villages. It was a Guernica of flesh and blood, and the shrieks were so filled with pain and hurt that they were almost unbearable. There were faces of anguish that looked up to God and pleaded for help. I saw Jimmy Constantine lying on the ground next to a twisted bicycle, screaming in agony.

"Now you see," he said. I stood in shocked silence.

"Now you understand," he shouted. He was angry. He filled the chapel with the darkness of his cloak, the red of blood, and the sound of pain. The folds of his clothing cloaked the faces of the statues and blotted out the light that had once illuminated the stained glass windows. He screamed with a loud cry that pierced the walls of the church with pain.

Then he was gone. Silence filled the church. I looked around at the stained glass, the carvings and the candles; I was alone. Death had vanished. I figured he was not leaving Erasmus empty-handed.

"No!" I screamed, the words coming up from the depths of my soul, desperate, very afraid. "No! Not again! You did the same thing to my brother! You did the same thing to Jamie!"

* * *

After my father left, I tried to talk to him. I walked into his room one night. The light was low and I could barely see him. He was cold and quiet and wrapped in his blanket.

"Jamie?"

"Yeah, Andrew?" he replied.

His eyes were tired. It was difficult for me to look directly into them. I had so many questions. How can I help you? What can I say to make this better? At what point did the stars no longer awe you, the cloud formations no longer fill you with wonder? I could tell that he hadn't been sleeping for a long time. I wanted to be able to lie on the floor in his bedroom and talk to him until he fell asleep, as before, to be like the sound of the rain on the roof that could lull him into peace.

"You want to talk?" I asked.

"Sure, Andrew," he would reply. "Just not now." I wrote him a poem and left it for him, after not now had become never.

When I was about ten, Jamie and I found a sick baby squirrel that had fallen out of its nest. We took it home and nursed it with eyedroppers of egg and milk.

"He belongs in the outdoors," my father said. "Much as you live in a house. He will be happiest with the other squirrels."

One day we brought the squirrel to the base of a tree, opened his cage door and let him go. He turned his head back to look at us, then scurried up the tree into the leaves. I cried but knew my father was probably right. The squirrel was going home.

After that I would see him now and then. I would walk out to the tree in the morning, and he would climb down to see me. Each day he seemed to climb down a shorter distance until one day he did not return at all.

Jamie was the same way. I saw him walk out the front door one day and head down the street. After that day I saw him less and less. We would stop on the street, say hello, chat a bit about nothing that was truly on our minds. Each time our talks became shorter. Eventually I rarely saw him at all. One time I thought I got a glimpse of him walking toward me on the street, haggard and shoulders sagging. The evening shadows helped obscure his identity.

"Jamie!" I yelled.

He stopped and looked at me. For a moment I thought he was coming toward me, but then he turned around and disappeared into the crowd.

The police called early one October morning. The night before hadn't been especially cold, but I don't think it matters. I think that there comes a point where your soul no longer finds any warmth in your body. Once that happens, even the slightest chill is enough to take a life, because the life is more than willing to be taken.

The police had found him a back alley nestled up to a dumpster. He had climbed inside a large cardboard box and was clutching a small stuffed animal that he had rescued from the trash. He had my poem in his pocket. He had made his choice, become part of the Big Dipper at last, the bear. Fear and disappointment were the hunters that were chasing him across the sky. I suppose he just got tired of running and allowed himself to be caught.

A few of our neighbors came to the funeral. Most hadn't really known Jamie. Though we had lived in that house for a while, Jamie had never been a constant there. I couldn't say I recognized most of the locals. It seems so often that we don't get time to say hello to people until we are saying goodbye to someone else.

Perhaps we had just been fortunate to have him in our family for the short time we knew him. I will never really understand what happened; never understand the world of drug addiction and self-destruction he had entered. I only knew that he was gone, and I could not follow. He had taken a dive into deep water, and I was still hanging onto the rope at the shore.

My mother didn't talk much after my brother died. We made a covenant in silence and pretended that our lives would move on, speaking of Jamie only now and then. It was a game, but somehow it just seemed harder to stop playing.

Eventually she followed my father and brother. I wasn't surprised. There was no one to talk to at the funeral because I was the only one to attend. At that point, I decided God was busy elsewhere. I could keep my promise to be like my uncle only if I did not expect any help from God. I was alone. I accepted that.

But not this time, I thought, *not now*. I was not going to let Death win again. He had taken his turn and now it was mine. I had to save Erasmus if I was to save myself. I was not going to give up so easily this time.

Chapter Thirteen

Rallying the Town

The church was staggeringly silent. Death had left an empty, cryptic stillness in place of the numbing scenes that he'd displayed only moments before. The walls surrounded me, ominously enclosing, but not offering sanctuary from fear. I was alone.

No, I repeated to myself, Death is not going to win this hand. I sat quietly while Jamie and others drifted away and then left the church. At the Constantines' house, I saw Jimmy's crumpled, twisted bike lying next to a makeshift ramp set up beside the house. People were taking covered dishes in through the front door. I saw Mrs. Davenport as she arrived with a purchased bucket of fried chicken.

"I'm not much of a cook," she said, ruefully.

"I'm going back to the hospital," I told her. Maybe there I could prevent Death from achieving his goal.

"No," Mrs. Davenport answered insistently. "You're needed here, Andrew."

"Why?" I asked.

"The storms are getting worse again. There's been a severe weather advisory. We may need to open the church as a shelter."

I hesitated. I wanted to go to the hospital. But maybe Death was just trying to break me away from Erasmus. Death was taunting me. He knew that the deadline had not been reached. He was getting worried because things were going in my direction.

"Okay," I said. I looked at my watch. Erasmus had little more than twenty-four hours in which to find faith. It was going to be close. I was certain that Death was not going to cut me any breaks. The storms were a bad sign and a possible portent to the destruction that would come with them.

Agnes joined us from the direction of the hospital.

"How's Jimmy?"

She sighed. "Hanging in there, for now."

"Okay," I responded. I stopped. "I think I've pretty much been preparing for this all my life."

Agnes and her mother gave me a quizzical look. "What do you mean?"

"I really can't explain. It's just that Death has been stalking me all my life in some form or another." The death of my uncle's faith. The death of my parents' relationship. The death of my brother and mother. I had been chased by Death since I could remember. It was only now that I was willing to turn around and face it.

The mystics gathered round us.

"I saw him again," I said.

"Saw who?" asked Agnes.

"The Angel of Death," I replied.

"Where?" she asked.

"In church," I said. "He was terrifying."

"Agnes and I will get the word out," Mrs. Davenport said.

"We'll help," the mystics said in unison.

"Agnes," I said, pulling her aside. "He's serious. I can feel it. These storms. . . ."

"These storms are common here."

"I'm not so sure," I said. "We're going to have to do better."

She was silent. I looked around me. It was a motley group at best. "We don't have much time," I called out. "We need to get everyone into the church."

They spread out in different directions, calling on the town to gather at the First Church of Erasmus. I ran to open the doors.

* * *

"Good afternoon, people of Erasmus," I said to the packed congregation. The Davenports and mystics had gathered the citizens, and the church was full. "As members of a community we are called together at times at times to celebrate, sometimes to mourn, and today we are called to pray.

"A reading from Ecclesiastes 3:1:

> "There is a time for everything, a season for every activity under heaven. A time to be born and time to die, a time to plant, a time to harvest, a time to kill and a time to heal."

I looked out over the congregation. There was a consistent, concerned look on their faces. Some fidgeted with their hands or with Kleenexes in their laps. Others were crying. A few looked serious.

"But it is also written in Ecclesiastes, that there is a time to tear and a time to mend, a time to be quiet and a time to speak up." I paused. "I have been quiet long enough."

A few people leaned forward to hear me better. Others looked up from the distractions they had been involved with. Agnes looked worried.

"When I arrived in Erasmus I encountered the Angel of Death. I warned this congregation last week that Death had picked this town to be destroyed. I was not lying. The proof now is with a boy. He is the warning. The storms are coming to destroy you."

"No!" someone shouted.

"Yes," I said.

The congregation was silent. A few people dabbed at wet eyes. Others looked surprised. Many looked skeptical.

"I have dedicated my life to having faith in God," I said. "Time after time I have been disappointed. Do you believe God cares? Maybe not. Maybe not for me, not for Jimmy Constantine, and not for Erasmus."

Agnes stood up. "You are wrong, Andrew. Listen to yourself. You speak of fear, not faith. Fear is weak. It will not be fear that saves us or this town, but the strength of our own faith."

I bowed my head in recognition. She was right, of course. I was allowing bitterness back in and, what was worse, speaking it aloud.

"Tomorrow is Erasmus Day," I said, softly now, so the congregation had to remain silent to hear. "You all know in your hearts if you have lost faith." There was a general murmured assent. "Even if you do not believe me, do not believe the Angel of Death will return to destroy the town if you do not repent, you still must do so, or you will be destroyed from within."

Mrs. Carstairs stood. "I trace my lineage on one side to Betsy Ross, and on the other to Levi Strauss," she said.

How had we gotten back on ancestry? "And that makes me the equivalent of seamstress royalty! I can make sackcloth outfits for this town. Who will help?" Several hands went up. *God bless you, Mrs. Carstairs,* I thought. It seemed that what little musical ability she possessed would be made up in sewing talent. I was blessed to have her Singer on my side.

"We can make signs," called Harpo. The mystics nodded in unison.

"We'll work all night!" said Lucy.

"Food's on me," called out John Luther Zwigli. "Anyone who needs anything, just stop by the Instant Coffee Cup. We're open for business!" Mrs. Davenport smiled in agreement.

"There's not much time," I hollered above the din. "Let's get going!" The people streamed from the church, headed to their different tasks. I set out to do the same. I knew what was needed tomorrow, the final element that would make the town repent. Something they could see: Annie Cotter.

I ran to the Instant Coffee Cup. The signs were down, the tape was gone. The door was unlocked. Someone had been replacing the pictures on the walls.

"Hello," I shouted. "Anyone here?" All was quiet. I walked down the back stairs and knocked lightly on Simon's door. It opened immediately. Simon looked different. His face was drawn and his clothes were ripped. In the light outside his dark room, he seemed thinner and grayer.

"Prophet, I must talk with you."

"What is it, Simon?" I asked.

"It's Annie."

"She's the reason I came to talk to you," I said hurriedly. "We need her tomorrow. The townspeople must have something they can see, to renew their faith. Please, Simon. You know I wouldn't ask if it wasn't urgent. This is life or death."

"No."

"Simon! The town will be destroyed!"

"A long time ago, when Annie died, this town lost its faith. They needed something to believe in then, too. Something they could see. My ancestors looked for a way. . . ."

"But when she didn't decompose," I said, "they had found a way."

"That's not true, Prophet."

"What do you mean?"

"We built her. She's fake."

"What?" I asked, stunned.

"We never let anyone near enough to see. But now, we need to tell the people the truth." I stared at him for a moment and could feel the fear encasing my body. "No," I said. "We will tell no one."

"Why?"

"Because it will only scare them to know."

"The truth will frighten them?" he asked.

"Look," I said, livid, "you fooled them for years. That's not my fault. But you're not going to mess things up now. Do you understand?" I loomed over him. He shrank back like a terrified child. "I am the prophet. I got God to send that storm. I will fix this. Don't say anything to anyone." Simon retreated into the shadows. I heard his footsteps on the Rice Krispies.

When I got back outside, clouds were slowly covering the stars and moon. An odd light emanated from the church. I noticed a figure hovering on the cupola. His long wings now extended out to the sides of his body, and light radiated from his eyes. The Angel of Death had returned.

* * *

I couldn't sleep. What Simon had said troubled me. I lay awake until early morning, angry with him for maintaining a lie and for causing a problem when we seemed so close. Perhaps that was why the Angel of Death was watching. Maybe he thought we were doing well. Erasmus Day was tomorrow. The whole town would come together for the event. It was our chance.

As I walked onto the Erasmus recreation field, I could see that the mystics had been busy. Booths were set up and the crowds were already arriving. The mystics were parading with their signs. Curly's read, "The end is near!" He was followed by Lucy, whose sign, "That's what Death Meant!" was waving energetically. Mae's read, "But we can change, there's still time!" John Wayne was holding one that said, "So repent,

repent." Lou Costello's "Only 235 more shopping days until Christmas," stood out in the crowd; I think he'd missed the point.

"Looks good," I told Harpo, who seemed to be organizing things. It was true they weren't funny anymore, but then the situation required seriousness, not laughter.

"Thanks," he said. "We worked all night."

"Look over there," Lou said and pointed. I could see chickens wandering around in a pen, pecking at their small burlap outfits. A cow roamed aimlessly near them. It was also wearing burlap. If nothing else, the livestock seemed to have a good case for being allowed to live.

"I'm going to walk around a bit, see how things look," I said, though overall I was feeling pretty satisfied. The town was starting to respond. Maybe, just maybe, Erasmus would be saved. I looked for the Angel on the church cupola, but the space was empty. Maybe he had moved on.

"I think I was wrong," John Wayne said as he leaned over to me. "I think maybe this time Harpo's speech might work."

"I sure hope you're right, John," I replied.

I walked out on the field to check out the booths. Mrs. Davenport's "Gates of Graft" had been commandeered by the local Boys' and Girls' Clubs. I paid the three extra dollars to set off the alarms. It was fun but somehow lacking the strangeness of what it was like to go through them when they were functioning for real.

Nate Auberjean had a stand set out to sell his famous eggplants. He also had a big stack of recordings by Florence Foster Jenkins. The Women's Group had a large table for their bake sale. The Men's Club, in an attempt to be politically correct, also had a bake sale, but their items looked less appetizing. The men probably hadn't looked at the directions.

There were tables set for plant sales. I saw row after row of yard sale items. In a town this size, it was really only a matter of trading. The next year the item would be resold to the original owner.

The Erasmus Historical Society had a table with a display of the history of Erasmus. There was also a picture of Annie Cotter. Mr. Cartwright sat behind the table. He looked at me and pointed to the picture of Annie Cotter.

"That's who you need out here," he said. "Annie Cotter."

"Seems like we're doing okay," I said, as a couple wandered by in sackcloth.

"Yeah, well, you'd be doing a whole heckuva lot better if she were here," he said.

"I think we'll do okay," I said.

"Thinking won't help. You can think *I'm a millionaire* but it won't make it true."

"We don't need her," I said, almost shouting.

I looked out over the field. Mrs. Carstairs' work was beginning to pay off. At least half the town was wearing sackcloth. Once everyone was attired in burlap, we would start working on lamentations. Those would come after the parade, which had just started.

Mrs. Davenport was the Grand Marshal. This was no different from any other year, except that this time she hadn't threatened the committee with their jobs. This time she had earned the honor.

The mystics continued working the crowd. Mrs. Carstairs had sewn until she dropped, and other ladies were passing around burlap garments. I had a speech to make. It was beginning to feel like we would succeed.

"Hey, Andrew." I heard my name and turned to see Agnes standing behind me.

"Hey, Agnes." Shyness welled up. I hated it.

"It's going well," she said.

"I hope so," I said.

"What do you mean?"

"I saw the Angel of Death again last night. I can't help thinking he's watching Erasmus still."

"Maybe he just needs to be sure."

"I don't think so," I said. I wanted to tell her about Simon, but I wasn't sure how she would respond. Would she believe me?

Agnes and I walked around the Erasmus Day Fair. We threw sponges at Mr. Dickinson from the First Bank of Merit. We danced to music composed solely for the kazoo, which was known as the Erasmus instrument of choice. We ate cotton candy that was sold by the Optimists' Club and unfortunately made of actual cotton. The Optimists' Club had been a bit too optimistic.

As we walked back to the street, Mrs. Carstairs approached us. She looked exhausted.

"Andrew, here is your shirt. I've even smudged some dirt on it."

"Thank you, Mrs. Carstairs. It looks sufficiently awful," I said.

She smiled at the compliment. "And yours will be next, Agnes."

I put the shirt on. It felt rough, like the time I put too much starch in my clothes. It was annoying, nothing more.

The Erasmus Day Fair was coming to an end. The townspeople were clearing up the tables and piling the trash into bins. The Women's Bake Sale proudly announced the success of its sale, the Men's Group had gotten lost on the way to the podium, and the Optimists' Club had changed their name to Pessimists'. John Luther Zwingli was wheeling a cart of food. Simon followed after him. I grabbed his shoulder. "Say nothing," I warned him sternly. He just gazed back at me blankly.

The mystics and John Luther Zwigli began herding people into the stands. A small podium had been set up with a microphone. Once all the townspeople had all gathered and were seated, I walked to the podium to begin my address, but Horace Bogardus got there first.

"Ladies and Gentleman," his voice boomed from the loudspeaker system. "Mrs. Davenport would like to thank everyone for pitching in and helping out during the fire at the Deep and Grubby. She pledges to keep paying everyone until we have the D&G up and functioning again!" A loud cheer went up from the crowd. I cringed.

"How could they just forgive her?" I whispered to John Luther Zwingli, who was standing next to me and cheering as well.

"How can they not?" he asked.

"But you? She tried to close you down!" I reminded him.

"That was yesterday, Andrew. If I fight all of yesterday's battles today, I will never have time to enjoy life."

"Well I guess she got what she deserved. The place is nearly destroyed," I stated.

"Why are you so bitter?" he asked. "Let it go."

"I'm not bitter. I guess I'm just confused." God had answered my call for help and I had defeated Mrs. Davenport. Still, I didn't feel satisfied. We still weren't safe. People hadn't even been receptive to the idea that I had a hand in the destruction of the Deep and Grubby—they said a storm was just a storm.

"Besides," he continued, "you should really be spending your time thinking about another member of the Davenport family."

Horace left the podium and graciously signaled for me to take it. I walked to the microphone.

"Faith," I said. "What good does faith do?" As I spoke I noticed, out of the corner of my eye, Simon and the mystics wheeling a glass coffin onto the field.

"Excuse me for one moment, ladies and gentlemen!" I said urgently, then climbed down and ran to Simon.

"Take her away!" I hissed angrily.

"Andrew," Harpo said. "This has nothing to do with Erasmus." The mystics, Simon, and John Luther Zwingli started to surround me.

"Stop it!" I told them. "Listen to me."

"We are listening," Simon said.

I turned on him. "You are a liar," I said. "You are destroying Erasmus."

"Andrew, what are you talking about?" Lou asked.

"He lied to us," I said, pointing at Simon. "Annie's a fake."

"Wait, Andrew," John Luther Zwingli said. "There is an explanation."

"Yes, there is," I said. "He's a liar!"

"Andrew, be fair."

"I'm tired of being fair. I'm tired of being lied to."

"Andrew," John Luther Zwingli grabbed my shoulder. "We all knew."

"You knew?" I asked.

"Yes, Andrew," he said. "We knew." The mystics nodded in agreement. "Simon wanted the town to believe so badly. It didn't do anyone any harm. We never needed Annie to have faith."

"Then you lied to me too. I trusted you. Even as a child I believed you. I laughed with you. But it was just a trick. I should never have listened to you, never believed in you."

John Luther Zwingli reached out to me. I pushed him away. I could tell he was surprised, but I didn't care. "You don't get it," I said. "We are going to fail. I came here to save Erasmus."

"No," he replied. "You came here to warn Erasmus, and you did that."

"And what good did it do?" I questioned.

"We don't know yet," he said. "But we still have time. But if we spread fear and hate, we will destroy ourselves long before Death comes."

"You think I'm spreading fear?" I asked.

"Yes," he said.

"It's my duty," I said. "I made a promise."

"You kept your promise. You warned us."

"It's not enough," I said.

"Andrew, you are prophet, you are not God."

I looked around. A crowd of people had now gathered around. I could not stay and wait while Erasmus was destroyed. The one truth they'd held onto, the faith they had placed in the miracle of Annie, was all a lie. I had been witness to the self-destruction of too many people in my life. The only difference this time was that I wouldn't have to watch. I looked at the faces of the crowd in front of me.

"You don't understand," I shouted. "You don't know Death like I do!"

"Andrew!" I heard people call out behind me, as I ran from the field.

Chapter Fourteen
Alone in the Wilderness

In my apartment I repacked my backpack, hoisted it on my back, and walked out into the night. The wind was beginning to pick up, and the rain was starting to fall. I could see formidable storm clouds grouped above me. The treetops were swaying wildly in the wind.

Main Street was deserted. I looked over at the town recreation field. It was deserted now, and like the town, appeared empty of hope. The rain fell harder, and my thin raincoat was getting soaked. I pulled the hood up and water cascaded into my eyes. I found the sign for the trail that Agnes had shown me earlier. It would be quicker. Leaves were blowing on the ground, and I almost missed finding the trailhead.

I fished in my pack for a flashlight, pulled it out, and turned it on. The batteries were old and the light was weak. I stopped now and then to regain my footing. A few blossoms had fallen, and as they blew in the wind they almost glowed.

Atop the hill leading out of Erasmus, I looked behind me. I could still see a few lights marking the town. Each step distanced me, and each time I turned around there were fewer lights visible. The scene reminded me of the old television screens when they were turned off: the ball of light would slowly disappear into the gray oblivion. Erasmus was no different. It would vanish into the storm. They had lied to me, and in her way Agnes had been a part of the lie. It was too late to return. I had made my choice. Hopes that hang on changing the past are death to the present.

I passed a pond and came to a river and a waterfall. I could see a tall pine reaching up into the sky and tossing in the wind. Trying to cross the river, I slipped on rocks and fell in. I cursed the rocks, cursed the water. The trees around me now were dancing frenetically like cornstalks in a summer thunderstorm. Falling branches crashed nearby. My body was soaked, and I began to shiver. My feet were becoming numb. I fished in my pack for my wool sweater. It wasn't there. I had left it back in Erasmus. In my hurry and anger I had forgotten it. My food had been left back on the floor.

The trail was partially obscured, and I continually wandered off only to find myself blocked by branches. I followed another path only to find it dead-ended by briars.

"Just get me out of here," I shouted. All I could think about was how angry I was. Everyone had lied to me in some way. I had cared about them.

Finally I stumbled into another patch of briars, fell in, and just lay there with the thorns against my hands and face. I started crying. My flashlight rolled into the underbrush.

"Stop playing with me," I screamed.

My jacket ripped as I pulled myself up. I stumbled back onto the trail. Soon I'd come to the meadow near the bridge. Once over it, I would be able to make a shelter by climbing into the dumpster behind the Quik Clean. I'd wait out the storm there.

I quickened my pace. I could hardly feel my toes anymore. A loud, watery crashing sound echoed nearby. I was not near the meadow. I was back at the waterfall. I'd been walking in a circle.

"Why are you doing this to me?" I shouted. "Why?" The river was now flowing full force. As I stepped out, I slipped again on a rock and tumbled into the water, hitting my head against a rock. Finally I climbed out onto the lower shore.

"I'm tired of this," I yelled. "I'm tired of being hurt." I pulled myself up onto the shore. In a tiny pool of stillness, I could see my reflection. Wrinkles and pain marked the face that stared back at me. My eyes were sunk in the black of hopelessness. My face had become that of my Uncle Andrew.

"Why are you doing this?" I shouted. Professor Anderson's words echoed in my ears.

"What is your question?"

"I don't know," I shouted. "I don't know." Clarify. Synthesize. Be clear.

"Am I to blame?" The water crashed even louder nearby. I shivered in the cold, and I could hardly muster the desire to live. The answer appeared to be yes.

I stared down at the watery blackness. No stars were reflected there. Darkness had enveloped the woods and taken the sky with it. I could feel my body tighten. The skin constricted around me, and I could feel a stiffening of my joints. I could no longer move. Even my lips were paralyzed. I huddled, freezing, barely able to speak.

"What is the question?"

I didn't want to ask. I was terrified of the answer I would receive. I could feel every last pain of my life welling up. I remembered every cause for resentment I'd experienced. I could no longer contain the anguish and the sorrow I had kept hidden inside. What was my question?

"Do you love me?" I whispered.

I stared at the blackness of the water's surface. There was now one solitary speck of light reflected in the pond. It was Polaris. I stared for a moment, and then from somewhere deep inside I screamed loudly into the night, and like a sword my voice cut the silence. The sound rippled the water's top, brushed the blades of grass on the edge and soared over the treetops.

"Do you love me?" I'd asked this of my mother, when she was crying, asked it of the night sky, asked it of God, while my older brother lay dying. He had been unable to hear the response that came back. I would need to listen for us both.

"I love you."

The tall pine tree was suddenly illuminated in a blue glow. The light enveloped the tree and embraced the waterfall and extended its warmth, surrounding me and holding me safe. Warmth entered my body, and the electricity of life resonated throughout. The trees stopped moving, the rain subsided, and the night sky began to clear.

I can't give up, I thought. *I must turn back.* All of my life I had been afraid. Afraid of abandonment. Afraid of death. Most of all I had been afraid of life.

I had been lost for such a long time when I had gone looking for God. Perhaps Harpo was right: I should have stayed in one place and waited for God to locate me.

The stars returned to the night sky. The moon was waxing, slowly getting brighter. Its lighted side was facing out, no doubt gathering light from a wandering comet. I focused my gaze on the Big Dipper. The stars that represented the hunters appeared to be moving closer to the bowl of the dipper. *But stars can't move,* I thought. I traced the handle back to its end. For the first time since I was a child, I could clearly see the small stars at the beginning of the bowl. One of the stars was moving ever so slowly back toward the handle, and this was causing the other stars in the handle to move away.

Jamie had found his faith. He had turned around and was chasing the hunters, his fear and doubt, back through the sky. I could see Jamie's star burning brighter than ever. He was laughing again, and the sound was bringing me light. I knew, wherever he was, he was all right. Somewhere, I knew, Halley's Comet was keeping a careful watch throughout its orbit.

My tears fell easily for Jamie, my father, and my mother, and for the town of Erasmus. We share so much in common. We all had our dreams. We all wanted to feel important. We all want love and to be loved. We all hurt. I suddenly felt connected, and the connection felt stronger and better than it ever had.

I had hated God for so long. I had been angry, and my anger had only continued the process of death. Long ago I had allowed my spirit to die, and it was only by the faith of a small boy, the belief of a town, and the magic of the night sky, that I had been resurrected.

The sweet fragrance of the grass surrounded me. The spring peepers' song drifted up from the pond. The rain was over, and the warm spring hovered over the tops of the plants. I lay back down, my hands underneath my head, and I lost myself in the depths of the Cosmos. I continued to sob; my heart opening, the bitterness and anger were replaced by a feeling of great love. One last gentle drop of rain touched my head. God was crying also.

The last noise I heard was the sound of voices surrounding me in the darkness. lights of varying shapes and sizes were coming through the woods.

"He's over here!" Leaves rustled under the trampling of feet.

"Andrew," someone said, "Andrew." I did not even feel my body being lifted and carried back down the trail.

Chapter Fifteen

Death Comes at Sunrise

I woke slowly. My body tingled, but the aches of the night were gone and warmth enveloped my skin. But I was uncertain of my surroundings. I gazed through heavy eyelids and could barely make out the walls. The bench cushions supporting me were familiar, and I could see the stained glass windows of the Erasmus Church. The windows were illuminated, and the saints depicted in them were aglow with the soft lunar light.

Standing up, I could see the church was filled with the sleeping townspeople of Erasmus. Mrs. Constantine and her oldest and youngest boys were stretched out in the front row. Mrs. Davenport was in the back, asleep in a chair. Harpo was snoring on the floor next to his harp as if he'd fallen asleep while playing, lulling the townspeople and himself with soothing music. Everywhere I looked there were blankets, sleeping bags, and prone figures.

I looked for Agnes and finally located her, lying on the back church pew, a small spread pulled up over her body. Her hair dropped over to one side. Her face was even more beautiful than I remembered. I wanted to brush the hair out of her eyes and kiss her, but I didn't want to wake her.

"Agnes, I whispered. "I'm sorry." I took a daisy from an arrangement by the pew and lay it next to her. "This," I murmured as I placed the flower next to her, "is so you know your prayers were answered."

I walked to the front door. Gentle light provided a guide through the stillness of the early morning. As I opened the door, I felt long fingers on my shoulder.

"Simon," I said. as I turned to face him.

"You are going."

"Yes," I replied. "I must."

"But your duty is finished."

"This isn't about duty. This is about love. Somehow, I know I must go."

"To?"

"To meet the Angel of Death," I replied. "Simon, I carry the faith of Erasmus in me. It exists. They believed in me, Simon. Even after I gave up on them."

"That is true," he replied.

"They kept their faith."

"And now you wish to return it."

"Yes. I know it is not over yet. I still feel his presence. Death is not finished with us."

He looked at me; his haggard gaze had been replaced with a caring look. His garments no longer looked torn and ragged. "You must do what you have to."

"I am sorry for losing faith," I said.

"But you returned to it. We all lose our way on the trail. All of us."

I was silent for moment. I wasn't sure if I would see Simon again. "Simon, if I don't return, please let them know that I am sorry," I said.

"I will, if you wish it."

"And tell the mystics they were right. Laughter heals."

"That is all?" he asked.

"No," I said. I stood in the silence of the church doorway. "Tell them that I love them."

"Ah. That is what I will tell them then. That you love them. The rest becomes unnecessary." He placed his hands on my shoulders. They were reassuring in the strength of their belief. Behind him, I could see the moonlight etched in the windows, the sleeping townspeople, and the open heart of the church.

I turned and looked out at the horizon. Dawn was approaching. I could hear the roosters crowing and could feel a slight breeze.

"Goodbye, Simon," I said.

Simon said nothing. He bowed as I walked down the steps of the church. I could see his gaunt silhouette still standing motionless in the church doorway as I walked up Main Street. He watched until I disappeared onto the trail.

My body tingled slightly, the now-familiar feeling increasing as I continued up the trail. The Angel of Death was waiting, and I knew from the compass in my body where I could find him. I looked down the trail behind me. The pond glimmered slightly, and a morning mist floated over it. I looked ahead. The trail wove up and over the hill.

I passed the waterfall. The gentle sound of the water was a comfort in comparison to the destructive power it had evinced only the night before. I threw a pebble into the water of the pool and watched the ripples.

I walked up through the meadow, accompanied by the songs of birds and the fragrance of spring flowers. Rabbits frolicked in the field, and I could have sworn one stopped and looked at me for a moment before hopping back into the grass.

In time I came to a road. It was Route 35, the same road that had brought me into Erasmus. The trail dropped not far from the bridge. The sun was just beginning to climb up over the horizon.

The sensations in my body were growing stronger. Death was close. As I drew nearer to the bridge, I saw a dark figure standing on the other side. His black garb rustled quietly in the gentle breeze. He began walking with certainty toward me.

I looked back over my shoulder. I could run away, but I knew it would only be a short time before I would have to return. I was meant to be here. Why? I still did not know. All I knew for certain was that I had to keep my faith.

Death headed straight toward me. I paused for a moment. I had made a decision in the night that I was now ready to keep. I would walk fearlessly toward Death. I was no longer afraid. I was prepared to die.

He stopped a few feet away from me. I looked into his face in hope of some sense of grace. His face was still. He had a determination of purpose.

"I am here," I said. "I am not afraid."

Death did not respond.

"I don't know if God believes in me," I said. "But I do know that I believe in God." Death listened solemnly as I spoke.

"And I have faith in Erasmus."

Death stood silently facing me. There was a profound sense of peace inside me. The buzzing and charge that had been so strong inside my body had now disappeared.

"You can't destroy Erasmus," I said. "I won't let you. I love them. You can destroy me."

The dark figure in front of me towered over my small frame. I saw him reach into the side of his cloak and remove a bright sword. The morning light connected with the blade and reflected off it. Death lifted the sword high in the air, and I expected it to land quickly. I had a short moment to catch a view of the weapon as it was brought up overhead. The polished metal served as a mirror. I could see my face in the blade. My reflection was no longer that of a bitter and angry man, but that of a boy who had promised not to give up, a boy had who sought and received God's love.

I waited in silence for the blade to connect. I had time to look out at the bright orange rising sun as it breached the horizon. I waited. A bird sang, the river toppled over the rocks, and the warm touch of the morning breeze caressed my skin. The storms of the night had been replaced by morning calm.

I did not want to look up. Perhaps I had died already and was just not aware of it. I did not want to face that reality. Death was still positioned firmly in front of me. Finally I could wait no longer. I looked up. The Angel of Death was bowing in my direction. I bowed in response and waited in the silence until I felt called to speak.

"Why stop?" I asked.

The Angel of Death stared deeply into my eyes.

"It is not called for. There's always reason, and I no longer have reason."

"But the town?" I asked. "What will happen to Erasmus?"

"I will not destroy them," he said.

I stood facing Death, and a sudden surge of power coursed through my body. I had beaten Death! I had saved a town from destruction! Then, what had been a sense of power changed into a great feeling of love. I no longer needed to prove myself.

"You will not destroy them?" I verified, watching the cloaked figure turn from me and walk toward the opposite end of the bridge.

The Angel of Death turned slowly to face me. He was still an imposing figure, but I sensed a certain decorum.

"They were saved!" I shouted, triumphant.

"No," he replied. "They were not."

"What?" I cried in indignation.

"I never meant to destroy the town," he said. The voice that had once terrified me now had the calming sound of rain on the roof.

"Then . . ." I paused. I felt the touch of a breeze and the warm rays of the sun in a way that I never had before. There was a sweet smell in the air. There were stars shining in the sky somewhere, even if I could not see them.

"But then . . . why did you come here?" I asked.

The Angel of Death faced me directly from the other side of the bridge. I no longer looked at him with fear but rather with tremendous awe and admiration. His garments now contained great beauty and color as they billowed in the breeze. The words that he replied were clear. I will remember them when I am afraid or when I have given up.

"I had come for you."

Book Group Questions

Thanks for reading *Saving Erasmus*. I wrote the book while In Quaker Divinity School. It is as much my story as it is Andrew's, although in different ways. The idea of what it meant to save and the conflict around faith were a part of both stories. I grew up Quaker. My memories of a church were of Presbyterian Church and church camp. Once, with family friends at church, I remember singing about the Father, Son, and Holy Ghost. The Quaker songs I knew didn't use this term. (I thought they were talking about Space Ghost, a cartoon.). My mother was raised as a Presbyterian.

I wrote the book as a reflection of my own journey. My father got sick when I was 3, and from that point on I felt a call to "save" institutions. I can't tell you how many places I started work at, where within a short time, the leader would leave, die or get sick. I think life/God helps us look at patterns by repeating them. I was guided not only by the bible but also but what I found as truths in other literature. The Velveteen Rabbit is a story of transcendence. The Little Prince is a story of the sweetness and sadness of relationship.

The book is also the story of how we develop meaning and how deep within our history those meanings go. So, there is a layer of meaning under the symbols and icons, much like in our spiritual lives. I wanted to include some saints and an Incorruptible as I think they are fascinating. The lives of saints was often more colorful and interesting than it might seem.

Book Group Queries

What literature/pop culture do you see referenced? Church history?

What books have given you spiritual support? Movies? Shows? Where do you find truths outside of church?

Annie Cotter is a representation of faith "seen". Is this true faith? Did "Doubting" Thomas have true faith? Where do you find faith?

What is it to be a prophet? What if no one listens?

What does it mean to save someone? Can someone be saved by another?

Is it wrong for Andrew to want the more prestigious church?

Simon believes in is duty. Can one take this too far? How has humor helped you in your spiritual life? In difficult times?

What church/religious images do you see in Simon's goodbye to Andrew?
What do you think the significance of the bridge is? What would happen if Andrew crossed it?

Extra:

What happens at the end?

Hidden Easter Eggs

I wrote *Saving Erasmus* while I was in seminary at the Earlham School of Religion and after having moved to the small city of Richmond, Indiana. It was Fall of 2001, and I had moved from the Boston area to the Midwest, all after what seemed like a calling. A calling I neglected for a long time.

While at seminary I was reading the bible (completely for the first time) and studying church history. I was struck by how my life had not only been impacted by biblical messages but also by stories handed down through generations. I had also been impacted by pop culture figures-their messages and words had guided me in my life. I read Neibuhr's *Faith*, resonating with the thought that our spiritual journeys takes us into a community of believers, and then into our own relationship with divinity.

Saving Erasmus weaves church history, pop culture and religion together simply because they have all guided me. As a Quaker I believe in continuing revelation, and that revelation can be found anywhere, if we are aware and receptive. Humor has always been important in my life, providing me the space to breath when the world seems to be crushing down on me. Humor plays a pivotal part in this book. Ironically Desiderius Erasmus would write a satire called, *In Praise of Folly.* He is also quoted as saying, "In the land of the blind, the one eyed man is king".

We are each part of a story interwoven with other stories; stories that are layered with meanings and ripples from the past. When we can come together, tell our stories and listen to each other's stories, then we form community and way opens for life to bloom.

Some chapters have more than others! Enjoy.

Title:

Saving Erasmus is about saving the town of Erasmus. St. Erasmus is also referred to as St. Elmo. St. Elmo's Fire is referenced later in the book. Besides being a 1980's movie, it is also the light that surrounds ships in a storm, and is considered a good omen.

Chapter One: *In Which I Meet the Angel of Death*

Chapter Two: *The Road Less Traveled*

Saint Augustine's and Saint Monica's: Saint Monica is Saint Augustine's mother.

St. Euxpery: Antoine de Sainte-Euxpery is the authot of *The Little Prince.*

Monte Hall: Monty Hall was the host of "Let's Make a Deal.

Holscher Hall: Named after a musician friend of mine, Nathan Holscher.

Michael Servetus: Michael Servetus was essentially the founder of the Unitarian Church. He believed in God as one, as opposed to John Calvin, who believed in the trinity. Calvin being Calvin, he had Servetus burned at the stake.

Three Stooges/Trinity/Graumann's :The argument of whether to honor the Three Stooges with one footprint or three refers to the argument between Servetus and Calvin (and a host of many others through time).

Saint Benedict and Nettles: Saint Benedict, like many others, felt one way to connect to God was to inflict pain. Hence clothing like hair shirts. Benedict rolled in nettles at least once. Before He developed his rules for community, other monks tried to poison him.

Nag Hammurabi: The Dead Sea Scrolls

Chicago Cubs/World Series: When this book came out, the Chicago Cubs had never won the World Series, so this ball would be an impossibility.

Professor Roy Hinkley: The Professor in *Gilligan's Island.*

Elaine Robinson: Mrs. Robinson' daughter and Dustin Hoffman's love interest in *The Graduate;* they are on the bus ride after the wedding scene.

Chapter Three: *Pelted With Plagues*

The Lady or the Tiger: This is a classic short story by Frank Stockton in which a man must a choice of doors, Behind one is a tiger. Behind the other is a lady. The man who chooses is the princess's lover and is being punished because he is of a lower class. The princess knows what is behind each door.

Jonas Grumby: The skipper in *Gilligan's Island.* Gilligan's Island was supposed to show a microcosm of life, each character representing a certain type-though lacking in racial diversity. I consider Grumby to be like Falstaff, though that makes Gilligan out to be Prince Hal.

3 Hour Trip (tour): The expected length of the boat ride in *Gilligan's Island.*

Plagues: The plagues are in the order that they show up in the Book of Exodus in the bible.

Chapter Four: *Mrs. Davenport*

Betty and Veronica's: From the *Archie* comic book series

Zuzu's Petals: Youngest child of Jimmy Stewart in the movie, *It's A Wonderful Life.* The petals fall off a flower she has brought home. Jimmy Stewart puts them in his pocket. When he finds them later on, they are the sign that he is alive.

No Name Auto: An auto repair shop I took my car to in Norwood, Massachusetts.

Wittenberg wood: Refers to the door of the church in Wittenberg where Luther placed the Ninety Five Theses, setting the stage for The Reformation.

Treasury of Merit: Under the control of the pope, it allowed him to offer indulgences (which like Mrs. Davenport's church) which favored the rich.

Chapter Five: *The Night Sky*

St. Elmo's Fire: The light that surrounds a ship during a storm. Said to be St. Erasmus, it serves a comfort.

Chapter Six: *Touring Erasmus*

Saint Teresa of Avila's *Interior Castle*: A book which details the way to the divine through many levels in the soul, or interior castle. Vermin reside there among other animals.

Natty Gann: Refers to Disney movie about a girl who makes a long journey to re-unite with her father.

John Luther Zwingli: John Luther Zwingli's name is an amalgamation of John (Calvin), (Martin) Luther and (Huldrych) Zwingli's names. These three fought over the meaning of the eucharist-

hence John Luther Zwingli's parents fighting over the bread recipe.

Chapter Seven: *Sermon on Amount*

Velveteen Rabbit: The classic book by Margery Williams about becoming real.

Albert Camus: Philosopher who stated that he found an invincible summer inside even in the midst of winter.

Horace Bogardus: The wealthy man in *Bells of St. Mary's* who ends up giving money to rebuild the church. He is played by Henry Travers, who also plays Clarence Odbody, the angel in *Its A Wonderful Life.*

Burma Shave Ads: Famous rhyming ads seen along the highway. The Deep and Grubby has similar ads.

Chapter Eight: *Jimmy Constantine*

Jimmy Constantine

Chapter Nine: *A Prodigal Daughter Returns*

Simon the Templar: Simon Templar is better known in pop culture as The Saint. He is a detective.

Chapter Ten: *When is a Door Not a Door?*

Chapter Eleven: *Ninety-five Pieces on the Wittenberg Door*

Ninety Five Pieces: Refers to the Ninety Five Theses, which Martin Luther wrote and supposedly placed on the door of the church in Wittenberg. Luther was challenging the churches positions on such actions as indulgences. Luther's actions would cause the Reformation.

Daisy as symbol: As much as I was limiting Jesus in this book because I had met a number of people who had felt alienated by other's use of him, he found his way into the book. In the Middle Ages, the daisy represented the innocence of the Christ child. In this book, it represents Daniel, who is essentially resurrected at the end.

Chapter Twelve: *Death Gets Serious*

Chapter Thirteen: *Rallying the Town*

Chapter Fourteen: *Alone in the Wilderness*

Chapter Fifteen: *Death Comes At Sunrise*

CPSIA information can be obtained
at www.ICGtesting.com
Printed in the USA
LVHW030951250520
656398LV00004B/236